"Even if you lose a child, you dream that you still have his love,"

Gavin told Norah. "You go on dreaming even when everything seems against you. Because you believe, you see, in this mystical bond between yourself and your son that nothing in the world can break. And then you have a chance to get him back, and you picture how it will be—how he'll run to you crying, 'Daddy,' and you'll hug him and all the years apart will disappear." Gavin stopped and drew a shuddering breath. Norah was silent, regarding him with pitying eyes.

"But it isn't like that," Gavin went on at last. "He doesn't run to you. You're a stranger he won't even talk to, and some other man is 'Daddy.' And there's nothing you can do about it." He dropped his head onto his hands.

Norah had an almost overwhelming desire to enfold Gavin in her arms and heal him with the warmth of her body. It took all her strength not to reach out to him....

Dear Reader,

Blue skies, sunshine, the scent of fresh-cut grass, a walk on the shore—some summer pleasures are irresistible. And Silhouette Romance has six more to add to your list—this month's irresistible heroes who will light up your August days—or nights—with romance!

He may act like a man of steel, but this FABULOUS FATHER has a heart of gold. Years of separation had made Gavin Hunter a stranger to his son, yet he was determined to make his home with the boy. But with beautiful Norah Bennett standing in his way, could Gavin win his son's heart without losing his own? Find out in Lucy Gordon's *Instant Father*.

Our next hero can be found in Elizabeth August's own SMYTHESHIRE, MASSACHUSETTS. Ryder Gerard may have married Emily Sayer to protect her young son, but he never intended to fall in love. *A Wedding for Emily* weaves the mysterious legacy of Smytheshire with the magic of marital love.

No reader will be able to resist the rugged, enigmatic Victor Damien. In Stella Bagwell's *Hero in Disguise*, reporter Sabrina Martin sets out to discover what her sexy boss, Victor, has to hide. Sabrina always gets her story, but will she get her man?

For more wonderful heroes to spend these lazy summer days with, check out Carol Grace's *Mail-Order Male*, Joan Smith's *John Loves Sally* and exciting new author Pamela Dalton's *The Prodigal Husband*.

In the coming months, we'll be bringing you books by all your favorite authors, such as Diana Palmer, Annette Broadrick, Marie Ferrarella, Carla Cassidy and many more.

Happy reading!

Anne Canadeo
Senior Editor

INSTANT FATHER

Lucy Gordon

Silhouette
ROMANCE™
Published by Silhouette Books New York
America's Publisher of Contemporary Romance

SILHOUETTE BOOKS
300 East 42nd St., New York, N.Y. 10017

INSTANT FATHER

ISBN: 0-373-08952-X

First Silhouette Books printing August 1993

All the characters in this book have no existence outside the imagination of the author and have no relation whatsoever to anyone bearing the same name or names. They are not even distantly inspired by any individual known or unknown to the author, and all incidents are pure invention.

®: Trademark used under license and registered in the United States Patent and Trademark Office and in other countries.

Printed in the U.S.A.

Books by Lucy Gordon

LUCY GORDON

met her husband-to-be in Venice, fell in love the first evening and got engaged two days later. After seventeen years, they're still happily married and now live in England with their three dogs. For twelve years Lucy was a writer for an English women's magazine. She interviewed many of the world's most interesting men, including Warren Beatty, Richard Chamberlain, Roger Moore, Sir Alec Guinness and Sir John Gielgud.

In 1985 she won the *Romantic Times* Reviewers' Choice Award for Outstanding Series Romance Author. She has also won a Golden Leaf Award from the New Jersey Chapter of the RWA, was a finalist in the RWA Golden Medallion contest in 1988 and won the 1990 Rita Award in the Best Traditional Romance category for *Song of the Lorelei*.

Gavin Hunter On Fatherhood:

I guess I had to write to you, son. We don't seem able to communicate any other way. You won't talk to me. When I speak, you look at me with eyes that are blank, or puzzled, or even hostile—eyes that seem to reproach me for having been a bad father, although God knows I never meant to be.

I thought being a father would be easy, that loving you would be enough. But then, I thought loving your mother would be enough, and she left me, taking you away, and making another man your father.

When they both died I was sure you'd be mine again. But we'd been apart too long. You turned away and wouldn't speak to me. You still won't.

So now I have to learn to be a father all over again, to a ten-year-old son who doesn't want me. I know you secretly wish I'd go away and leave you with Norah, your stepsister, who has your heart. But I won't go, because I am still your father and I love you. When I seem cold and hard it is because loving you and getting nothing back hurts so much. Perhaps Norah has the key. Perhaps she can teach me. Who knows. I only know that I'll never give up hope....

Chapter One

"You've simply got to face facts, Gavin. The figures don't look good. Hunter and Son is rapidly becoming a paper company—splendid on the surface, but nothing behind it but debt."

Gavin Hunter's dark brows almost met as he frowned angrily. "Hunter and Son has always been good for any amount of credit," he snapped.

The banker, who was also a friend insofar as Gavin Hunter had any friends, pulled a wry face. "That was then. This is now. The great days of property are over. Interest rates rise as prices fall. Some of your hotels are only just hanging on. Since they're mortgaged to the hilt, it won't even help you to sell them."

"I don't want to sell," Gavin snapped. "I want a small loan to keep me going. A mere quarter of a million pounds. In the past you've loaned me four times that without blinking."

"In the past you had excellent collateral to back it up. Look, I'm not sure... What's the matter?" The banker had realized that Gavin was no longer listening to him. His attention was fixed on the television screen in the corner of the room. "Is that disturbing you? I have it on to catch the news, but I can turn it off."

"Turn the sound up," Gavin said hoarsely.

The screen was filled with a photograph of an amiable looking middle-aged man. The banker turned up the sound.

"*... died today in a car crash that also killed his wife, Elizabeth. Tony Ackroyd was one of the world's best-known naturalists, a man who'd been prominent in...*"

Gavin was gathering his things together, thrusting them hastily back into his briefcase. "Don't you want to talk some more?" the banker said.

"Not just now. I have urgent business to attend to."

The banker frowned, then enlightenment dawned. "Of course. Those two in the car crash—weren't they—?"

"Yes," Gavin said harshly. "They were my enemies."

As he headed north out of London he reflected that Liz hadn't always been his enemy. Once—and it was hard to imagine it now—he'd been in love with her, had swept her off her feet with his ardor and into a doomed marriage. In retrospect he understood that they'd never had a chance, although for a time they'd been happy, or so he'd thought. To all appearances they were a glorious couple, Liz with her long fair hair and ethereal beauty; Gavin with his dark good looks and his ability to turn whatever he touched into gold. They had a luxurious apartment in London, where Liz had given exquisite dinner parties. She was the perfect hostess and Gavin had been proud of her. She'd borne him a son, Peter, whom he'd loved with all the force of his proud, intense nature. He'd built his dreams around Peter, looking forward to the day when he would be the "son" in Hunter and Son.

But Liz had blown the dreams apart when she'd left him for Tony Ackroyd and stolen his four-year-old son. From that day she'd been his enemy.

He could still hear her crying, "I can't stand you any more. Business and money. Money and business. That's all you think about."

And his own reply. "I work for you and Peter."

"You're deluding yourself. You do it for yourself—and your father."

It was true he'd striven to impress his father, but that was because he had a lot to live up to. William Hunter had built up a hotel chain from nothing and reared Gavin in the belief that it was a son's duty to outstrip his father's achievements. He'd handed the business on with the implied demand for more, for bigger and better and bolder.

William was still alive, living in a convalescent home on the south coast, because that was the only place where his frail lungs could breathe. But his brain had stayed vigorous enough for him to bombard his son with a stream of letters containing unsolicited advice, most of it useless because his knowledge was out-of-date. Gavin had fielded the advice while expanding the business his own way. The strain had been considerable, but he'd trusted Liz to understand. And she'd failed him.

Cuckolded, he thought, taking a bitter satisfaction in the robust, old-fashioned word. Cuckolded by a sissy, a man with long hair and a beard, who went about with a vague air as if he didn't know what day it was—a man who talked to animals, of all things! "Tony's a better man than you," Liz had flung at him. But that had been just spite.

He stepped on the gas. He wanted to get as near as possible to Strand House before the light faded.

Strand House. He could almost see it before him, exactly as he'd first set eyes on it, the great eighteenth-century mansion looking out over the sea. As a boy William had worked there, doing carpentry for the aristocratic family who owned it. Later, when he'd made his fortune, it had been his dream to own the place. He hadn't succeeded, but Gavin did. The family had fallen on hard times and he'd badgered them until they sold up. The proudest day of Gavin's life had been when he could show William the title deeds in his possession. But even then William had found cause for complaint.

"Why isn't it in your sole name?" he'd snapped.

"For tax reasons, Dad," Gavin had explained patiently. "It'll be a lot cheaper if it's in Liz's name too. Don't worry. It's only on paper."

But it hadn't worked out like that. Liz had fallen in love with the house and the sea, wanted to make a home there. He'd explained that their home had to be in London.

"That's not a home," she'd told him. "That's just a base for exhibiting to people you want to overwhelm. I want a *home*."

Because he didn't understand her, he'd tried to pass it off as a joke. "Don't people say home is where the heart is?"

And she'd answered, in terrible bitterness, "That's for people who have hearts, Gavin."

He'd concealed his hurt and stood his ground. Strand House was going to be the jewel of the Hunter hotel chain. He had the plans all drawn up: the indoor swimming pool created from the huge conservatory, the sauna in what was now the billiard room, and the golf course that would occupy the grounds, making use of the beautiful lawns that the family had tended for centuries.

But before he could put the plans into effect Liz had run away, taking Peter. As a final twist of the screw she'd betrayed him once more, claiming "her" half of the house in the divorce settlement. He'd fought her to the last ditch, but he'd lost. The court had awarded her half of Strand House with the right to live there, provided she paid him rent for his half. It had also awarded her custody of Peter.

He'd driven through the night then, as he was doing now, and arrived at the house like a maddened bull. It was early in the day, but there was no sign of Liz or "that sponger," as he referred to Tony in his head. He'd charged through the house and out again onto the ground, searching madly, driven by a terrible fear that they'd taken his son abroad.

At last he'd found someone who looked like the gardener's boy, dressed in shabby jeans, sweater and an ancient hat, and digging a trench in the middle of a perfect lawn. He drew an angry breath at the thought of his ruined golf course. "Hey you!" he snapped. "What do you think you're doing?"

The battered hat had lifted and he found himself staring into the face of a young woman who couldn't have been more than eighteen. She had a curious face, not beautiful but full of life and personality, with a hint of humor lurking not far below the surface. Her only claim to good looks lay in her eyes, which were large, brown and warm. For the rest, her nose was too long, her mouth too wide and her chin too stubborn, yet the total effect was oddly pleasing. Or would have been, if Gavin had been in a mood to be pleased. Right now her mood seemed as belligerent as his own. "Are you talking to me?" she enquired.

"Yes I am. I asked what you thought you were doing to that lawn."

"I'm digging it up," she explained patiently. "What does it look as if I'm doing?"

"Don't give me any cheek. Do you know how many years it took to get that lawn perfect?"

"Yes, and it's about time somebody did something useful to it," she countered. "It's nice and sunny here. Ideal for vegetables."

He gritted his teeth. "Where's your employer?"

A faint smile that he hadn't understood until later flitted across her curved lips. "Do you mean Mr. Ackroyd?"

"Stop playing stupid—"

"I'm not playing," she declared innocently. "You'd be amazed how stupid I can be—when it suits me."

If he hadn't been so angry and upset he might have heeded the warning, but all he saw was that he was being thwarted again, something he always found intolerable, but now more than ever. "I warn you I'm losing my patience," he growled.

She nodded. "I can see that. I don't suppose you had much to begin with."

"Now look—"

"Do you usually go around shouting at people like an army sergeant? Should I jump? Stand to attention? Sorry. Can't oblige."

"Why don't you try a little plain civility?" he snapped.

"Why don't *you?* You storm into my home and start barking orders—"

"*Your* home? What the devil do you mean by that?"

"It belongs to the woman my father's going to marry, and we're all living in it together. Is that plain enough?"

"Yes, it's plain enough. And since we're going in for plain speaking, it's my turn. I take it your father is Tony Ackroyd, and the woman he's going to marry is Elizabeth Hunter, *my wife.*"

Her marvelous eyes widened, and the words came rushing out of her. "Your wife? Good grief! Grating Gavin!"

"I beg your pardon?" he said ominously.

"Nothing," she said hastily. "I didn't say anything."

"You said 'grating Gavin.' I should like to know why."

"Look, it's just a silly name . . ." she floundered.

"Are you telling me that my wife calls me that?"

"Of course not . . . not exactly . . . this is . . ."

"Does she or doesn't she? Or are you too stupid to know the difference?"

The color flew to her cheeks. "You're a real charmer, aren't you? All right, if you must know, Liz said everything you do grates on her, and I—"

"You invented the name," he finished. "And you have the nerve to lecture me about manners."

"You weren't meant to know about it. How could I dream you'd ever come here?"

"I came to see my wife. She still *is* my wife until the divorce is finalized, which won't be for another two weeks. Let me further make it clear that she doesn't own Strand House, only half of it. The other half belongs to me."

She frowned. "Only until my father buys you out, surely?"

"Buy me out?" he demanded with bitter hilarity. "Do you know what this place is worth? Of course you don't. I know your kind—and his. Floating through life on a 'green' cloud, with no idea of reality. There's no way your father could afford it, even if I were prepared to sell, which I'm not."

"What on earth can you gain by refusing to sell?"

"That's for me to say."

She stood back to regard him. "Oh, I see," she said cynically.

He knew it was unwise to continue this conversation. He didn't owe this impertinent urchin any explanation, and freezing dignity would be his best course. But he couldn't manage it. There was something provoking about her that drove him on. "What do you think you see?" he demanded.

"You're going to be a dog in the manger, aren't you? You can't have Strand House yourself, but you can make sure Liz can't fully enjoy it."

"Young woman, I don't know what you think gives you the right to make quick, cheap judgments without knowing the full facts, but let me tell you you're way out of line."

"Oh, the truth hurts, does it?"

"It isn't the truth."

"Oh, yes, it is. Why should you want to hang onto any part of this place, unless it's for the pleasure of making poor Liz miserable?"

"I'm hanging onto it because it's mine. She has no right to any part of it."

"That's not what the title deeds say."

"The title deeds are a formality for tax purposes, and Liz knew that perfectly well."

"If all your wife meant to you was a tax dodge, I'm not surprised she left you. She should have left you years ago."

"Another glib judgment made in ignorance."

"It's not my judgment, it's hers. Why don't you just let her go? Let my father buy you out."

"He couldn't do it in a million years. He only offers to buy me out because he knows there's no fear of my taking him up on it. He knew a good thing when he met Liz, didn't he? A rich woman who could walk away from her husband with a lot of property."

She paled. "How dare you speak about my father like that? He's an honorable man, and he loves Liz."

"Does he? Or does he love what she can bring him?"

"You've got no right to say that. You don't know him."

"I know he stole my wife, my house and my son. What else do I need to know?"

"He didn't steal your wife. He won her by offering her the love you couldn't, the only currency that counts, only nobody ever told you that, did they? If you'd known about love you might still have your wife, your house *and* your son."

"Don't tell me I don't love my son. I'll be damned if I'll let him be brought up by Tony Ackroyd."

"He'll be lucky if he is. There isn't a better father in the world."

"The best father is his own father."

"He's four years old, for pity's sake. How can you try to snatch a child so young away from his mother?"

Through the confused mass of pain and bewilderment that possessed him, he couldn't find the words that would express his true feelings. All he could manage to do was cry out, "Because he's *mine*."

It was the wrong thing to say. He wasn't so insensitive that he couldn't realize that. But no other words would come.

He saw her looking at him in contemptuous disbelief. "The house is your. Liz is yours. Peter is yours. It's all property to you, isn't it?"

"No, it isn't," he snapped. "Peter and I..." He stopped. It would have been hard enough to speak of his bittersweet love for his son with a sympathetic listener. With this judgmental young woman it was impossible. "Never mind," he said, unaware of how plainly his thoughts had been revealed on his face. "Just tell me where I can find my wife and son," he said.

Her eyes were fixed on his face, and they had a new look, as though she'd seen something that had startled her. Her manner softened. "They're inside," she said. "I'll tell them you're here."

She thrust her spade into the earth with a strong movement and ran back to the house. Gavin felt shaken and drained by the interview. He began to look around him and realized that the destruction extended much further than digging up a lawn. Tony Ackroyd evidently had big plans for the grounds, if the huge rolls of wire lying about were anything to go by.

"Daddy."

He turned to see his little son scampering across the lawn toward him. For a moment delight blotted out all other thought, and he opened his arms to scoop him up. The little boy's warmth sent a sensation of joy flowing through him. "Have you missed me?" he asked.

Peter nodded, smiling.

Gavin looked around. There was nobody about. Soon the angry young woman would rouse the house, but for the moment the coast was clear. He could escape now, taking Peter with him. "Peter," he asked in a low, urgent voice, "would you like to come home with me?"

His anxious eyes noted how the child brightened, and his heart began to beat with hope. "We've got so much to do together," he said. "We can go to the zoo and see the lions and tigers and—"

"Uncle Tony says it's wrong to keep lions and tigers behind bars," Peter said, frowning. "He says it's cruel."

Gavin took a deep breath. "All right, never mind the zoo. You can have that computer game you wanted. And we'll—"

"Can I have a puppy all of my own?"

"Well, that's not going to be easy, because our flat doesn't have a garden."

"But Uncle Tony says—"

"All right, you can have a puppy," Gavin said hastily. "Shall we go now?"

"Is Mommy coming, too?" Peter asked.

"No, just the two of us."

"But I want Mommy. I want *Mommy*."

In the silence that followed, he knew he'd lost. He was a hard man, but not hard enough to force a four-year-old child to leave his mother against his will. He sighed. "I guess that's that, then," he said.

"Are you going to stay with us?" Peter asked hopefully.

"No, I—I just came to see how you were."

"But I want you to stay."

"And I'd like to be with you but Mommy and I can't be together any more—"

"Why not?"

It would have been so easy to say, "Because she's a faithless wife who walked out and she's the one keeping us apart." Put the blame on Liz, where it belonged. Teach her son to blame her. See what she made of that.

But he couldn't make himself tear the child apart. He despised himself for a sentimental weakling, but he couldn't do it. "Because that's the way it has to be," he said with a sigh. "You and I will still see each other sometimes. As often as I can manage. I promise. Be a good boy for your Mommy and—"

Before he got the next words out a whirlwind seemed to descend on him, Peter was snatched from his arms and Liz was standing there before him, her face blazing. "I might have known you'd try something like this," she said furiously. "Another moment and you'd have spirited him away. Oh, thank God I got here in time!"

"Spare me the dramatics," he said coldly. "I was saying goodbye."

"It's a lie," she cried. "I know you. You were trying to steal him."

The angry young woman had hurried up behind Liz and was watching the little scene with a frown. "Liz—" she said.

"Did you see what he was trying to do?" Liz demanded. "If you hadn't come and warned us, he'd have got away with it."

"Liz, I don't think he was trying to—"

"Nonsense, of course he was. That's what he came here for."

"Whatever I came here for, it was plainly a wasted journey," Gavin said, tight-lipped. "I had hoped that we could talk reasonably, but you won't listen, so I may as well leave. Take good care of my son. Goodbye, Peter." He reached out to pat his son's shoulder, but Liz stepped back, taking him out of reach and began to run toward the house. Gavin tightened his lips against the pain and walked away to his car.

As he was getting into it he stopped for one look back. Liz had gone, but the young woman was still there, watching him and frowning as if something had puzzled her. He got in, slamming the door, and drove off. His mind was in too much of a whirl to think straight. It was only when he was miles away that he realized she had actually defended him.

After that visit things became more difficult. Liz had called her lawyer to report that he'd tried to abduct Peter, and although he still had access to his son it became very limited. On the rare occasions when they met Peter's manner toward him was awkward, and Gavin could only guess at how they'd tried to turn him against his father. As six years passed and the boy grew up, Gavin had felt with despair that he was losing something he could never regain.

But now everything would be different. Now there was nothing to stop him from reclaiming his son. Peter had suffered from divided loyalties, but that was over, and soon he would be close to his father again.

As dawn broke he could hear the sound of the sea in the distance, and his heart quickened at the thought that he would soon be there. He thought of how Peter would run to him as the only safe point in a world that had suddenly become chaotic. He wondered who would be with him. Probably Ackroyd's daughter. He knew now that her name was Norah, but she'd lived in his mind as the angry young woman. He wondered if she would try to stop him from claiming his child. If so, she wouldn't succeed. As he drove the last stretch he rehearsed the words he would say to her, strong words that would leave her in no doubt that he wasn't to be trifled with.

At last the house came in sight, pale and beautiful in the dawn light. He felt a surge of love for the place. His thoughts had been all of Peter, but now it occurred to him that the house too would revert to him, in a sense. Liz's share would pass to Peter, and as Peter's guardian he would hold his son's inheritance in trust. They would own Strand House together. He liked the sound of that.

There was no sign of life as he drove up the drive and stopped in front of the house. The light was already growing strong, but it was six in the morning. He got out of the car and looked up at the windows which showed no sign of life. He began to walk around the house to reach the extensive grounds that stretched away at the rear. He wanted to groan when he saw what had become of them. The perfect lawns that would have been the golf course had been dug up and now housed what appeared to be a small zoo.

He made his way between wire cages until at last he saw a figure sitting on a wooden bench. She was dressed in an old sweater and dark jeans, and she sat hugging her arms across her chest, staring into space.

A black-and-white dog who'd settled at her feet looked up at Gavin's approach and gave a soft, "Wuff." She glanced up at him without speaking and he recognized Norah. She was different. Her face was deadly pale and full of despair and she looked as if all the fight had been drained out of her. Suddenly the firm words he'd rehearsed vanished from his head, leaving only one thought.

He said gently, "I'm so very, very sorry. It must be dreadful for you."

Chapter Two

"It's you," she said, as if dazed.

"Weren't you expecting me after—what's happened?"

"I don't know—I haven't taken it in yet. It seems only yesterday that I waved them off...." She gave a little shudder. "It *was* only yesterday. And now the whole world has changed."

He sat beside her on the bench. "How is Peter? Does he know?"

"He knew before anyone else," she said huskily. "The worst possible thing happened. He was watching the news, and he saw it first. Nobody had called to warn us. It was a dreadful shock for him. He came and told me. At first I didn't believe him. I thought he'd misunderstood. He kept crying and saying, 'It's true, it's true.' Then we cried together for most of the night."

"It's a terrible burden for you," he said sympathetically. "But I'm here now."

She gave him a strange look which he failed to interpret, and said, "Peter fell asleep about an hour ago. I came out here because it's where I feel closest to Dad. We built all this up together. He loved it so much. He used to say all the money in the world didn't mean as much as an animal's trust."

Gavin thought that a man who'd attached himself to a rich woman was free to be indifferent to money, but it would have been cruel to say it to her, so he kept silent.

"They all trusted him," Norah said, looking around at the animals who were beginning to awake and appear. "How am I going to tell them?"

"Tell them what?" Gavin asked blankly.

"That he and Liz are dead," she said simply.

He stared at her. Nothing in his experience had prepared him to cope with someone who talked like this. Trying to hide his exasperation he said, "Surely there'll be no need to tell them."

Her frown cleared. "You're right. They'll know by instinct. I should have remembered that."

She looked at him with her head on one side, and he realized that she was wondering how he came to understand such a thing. He felt at an impasse. It irritated him to be misinterpreted, but he was touched by the grief so clearly evident on her face.

It was six years since he'd seen her and in that time she'd changed from an urchin into a woman. Her body had rounded out and her face had grown softer. It was pale now, and haggard and suffering, but some men would have found her attractive, he realized.

As he watched her he saw her expression change yet again, and she gave him a rueful look that was almost a smile. "I read you wrong, didn't I?" she asked. "You didn't mean that the animals would know. You meant, why bother to tell animals anything?"

Paradoxically he was even more disconcerted now than he'd been a moment ago. "Well," he said awkwardly, "after all, they are only animals."

She sighed. "Dad spent his life trying to open the eyes of people who thought like that."

"I doubt he'd have converted me."

"No, I don't suppose he would. But that wouldn't have stopped him trying. He said you should never give up on anyone, no matter how—" she stopped.

To divert her attention he asked, "If he felt like that, why did he keep a zoo?"

"It's not a zoo, it's a sanctuary. Most of the creatures here were brought in because they were sick or ill treated. We try to get—that is, the idea is to get them well enough to return to the wild."

He felt relieved. He'd been wondering how to break it to her that she must close down the place and leave. Now he saw that it could be done gradually as the animals were released. He had no desire to be brutal.

"Let's go inside," she said. "I'll make us some coffee."

The dog rose at the exact moment she did and kept close to her as they walked. She led him up to the house and through the french doors that led into the big sun lounge at the back of the house. He stared at the change he found. The beautiful eighteenth-century furniture had all gone, replaced by functional pieces that looked as if they'd come from junk shops. Some of them were completely covered in sheets on which a variety of creatures lay snoozing. There were dogs and cats, a parrot and a monkey.

"The good furniture is stored at the top of the house," Norah said, reading his look. "It would have been a pity to let it get dirty."

"Quite," he said wryly.

The animals were awakening and beginning to crowd around her. She scratched their heads and caressed their coats, seeming to take comfort in the very feel of them. "The sanctuary doesn't officially take cats and dogs, because there are so many other places for them," she said, "but they seem to arrive anyway. People bring them, and there are a couple who made their own way here. It's almost as if they knew where to come."

Gavin said nothing. Her approach seemed to him so outrageously whimsical that it was better to hold his tongue. He thought of his son being reared in this atmosphere, and thanked a merciful heaven that he'd been allowed to rescue him in time.

The kitchen had also altered beyond recognition. He'd last seen it when it was charming and old-fashioned. Now it closely resembled the deck of a spaceship, and in this he recognized Liz's handiwork. She'd been an avid cook, complaining bitterly when he arrived home late and her creations were ruined.

"This was Liz's dream," Norah explained, apparently reading his thoughts again in a way that was becoming unsettling. "She loved having every modern gadget she could find."

"But this looks like a hotel catering oven," Gavin protested, regarding a shiny monster, all knobs and lights.

"It is. She got it because the animals need so much food. She used to do huge batches of cooking and store it in the freezer."

"*Liz* cooked for animals?"

He thought of the elegant, sophisticated woman who'd once been his wife, thought of the Cordon Bleu dishes that had been her expression of artistry. But "they" had got to her. She'd fallen into the clutches of Tony Ackroyd and his daughter, and this was the result.

Norah put on the coffee, then turned her attention to a small hedgehog in a box in a corner. "She let you keep animals in her kitchen?" Gavin asked.

"It was Liz who brought Bert in here," Norah said, setting down a saucer of milk for the hedgehog. "He's very frail and he needs warmth. She loves—loved—the animals as much as Dad and me."

"Hmm. I doubt that. She wasn't exactly an 'animal' sort of person."

"What sort of person was she, then?" Norah looked at him curiously, and he scented a trap.

"It hardly matters now, does it?" he said.

"No," she whispered.

She turned away from him with her head bent and her shoulders shaking. But almost at once she straightened up. He thought he saw her wipe a hand over her eyes and when she next spoke her voice sounded a little muffled, but she'd recovered her composure. "How did you hear about their deaths?" she asked.

"On the television news. I came straight here."

"And you've driven through the night? You must be tired. I'll fix you a room."

"I'd rather see my son as soon as possible."

"Of course. But don't wake him now. Let the poor, little soul have a good sleep."

She poured him and herself some coffee. As they drank they each felt a constraint fall over them. In the surprise of seeing each other they'd behaved naturally, but now it seemed strange that they should be sitting here talking together. "What actually happened?" Gavin asked at last. "I didn't gather much from the news."

"It happened in a country lane. Apparently a farmer saw everything, and he said a rabbit ran out onto the road—"

"Are you telling me that your father killed Liz to avoid a rabbit?" Gavin demanded sharply.

"Liz was driving."

"You can't possibly know that."

"It was her car. Dad had just given it to her. She loved driving it whenever she could. And the farmer saw her at the wheel. He said she was going too fast to stop, and when the rabbit appeared she swerved and—and they overturned."

"He gave it to her?" Gavin echoed. "What kind of car was it?" Norah told him. It was the latest version of a fast, powerful make. "What did he think he was doing giving her a car like that?" Gavin demanded angrily.

"It was the one she wanted. He tried to talk her out of it, but Liz was adamant that it was that or nothing. She promised she'd be careful but—she loved going fast."

His rage was growing. "He must have known that. He should never have given in."

"Stop it," she said desperately. "Stop trying to find excuses to make everything Dad's fault."

"I know that before she met him she'd never have risked her life to avoid a rabbit. That was his doing, and but for that she might be alive."

Norah raised her voice so as to be heard above his rage. "Gavin, my father was not to blame for every single thing that's gone wrong in your life and hers."

The pain he'd been repressing broke out. "I suppose such an insane act makes perfect sense to you, doesn't it?" he snapped.

"If you mean would I have swerved to avoid hitting an animal, yes, I would. But I never drove as fast as Liz, nor did Dad. If either of us—"

"It wasn't her fault," he shouted. "Before she lived with you and your father she was a woman of common sense, but the two of you seem to have sabotaged her mind."

"That's wickedly unfair—"

"Good God, what a household for my son to grow up in! All I can say is the sooner I remove him from your pernicious influence, the better."

He stopped because he could see he'd lost her attention. Norah was staring over his shoulder at the doorway. Turning, Gavin saw Peter standing there in pajamas. His heart was suddenly full of joy and relief. What did anything else matter beside the reunion with his beloved son?

"Hallo, son," he said gently, holding out his arms.

But Peter didn't run into them as he should have done. Instead he stared at Gavin with wide, dismayed eyes, before rushing past him to Norah. Gavin watched, incredulous, as Peter flung himself into Norah's arms and buried his face against her. He noticed how her arms closed protectively around the child. The two of them stayed locked together for several seconds.

"Your father came to see you, darling," Norah whispered. "You should at least say hallo to him."

But Peter refused to turn around, and Gavin thought he heard a muffled cry of, "No! no!"

"Everything's happened a bit suddenly for him," she explained apologetically to Gavin.

"Thank you, I don't need my son explained to me," he said coolly. "It's quite clear what has happened. You mentioned a room. I'd be glad of the chance to settle in."

"Of course." Norah gave her attention back to Peter. "Darling, I want you to go outside and see if everything's all right. Some of the animals are a bit unsettled. Calm them down, the way you do."

"Do they know?" the boy choked.

"Yes," she said quietly. "I think they know. I believe some of them may have known before we did. Go on, now."

The boy scuttled out without looking at Gavin, who turned furious eyes on Norah. "It's as well I came when I did—filling my son's head up with that kind of tomfoolery. Knew before we did! I never heard anything like that."

"Some of them got very agitated early yesterday evening," Norah replied. "They started calling out in ways I've never heard before and tearing around their pens. We couldn't understand it. But I know it was about the time of the crash."

"Coincidence," Gavin snapped.

"Perhaps. When someone discovers exactly how their senses work, maybe we'll know. I'll show you upstairs."

He'd slept in the house for a week after he'd bought it, lying in the great master bedroom and reveling in making plans which had come to nothing. As they reached the top of the stairs he turned instinctively toward the door of that room, but Norah steered him away. "That's where they slept," she said. "It's full of their things."

"Of course," he said curtly, and followed her down the corridor to a room at the end.

"This is always kept made up for guests," she explained. "This door here is your bathroom. It's been put in since you were last here."

"Thank you." It was hard not to resent her proprietory air. With an effort he stopped himself from pointing out that this was his house and she was the guest, and moreover a guest who would soon be departing. He was glad when she left him alone.

The room looked out over the grounds. Standing at the window he could see Peter moving among the animals, stroking them, resting his head against them. He feasted his eyes on his son. He loved him so much, and it was wonderful to have him back at last.

But did he have him back? He was suddenly dreadfully conscious of the distance between them. And his son hadn't run to him, but to Norah. He'd stared at his father with the eyes of a stranger and almost seemed to shrink from him.

No! Gavin stopped himself on that thought. His son hadn't shrunk from him. He'd merely been taken by surprise. But they would put it right, just as soon as he could remove Peter from this place and have him to himself. And that was going to be at the first possible moment.

He found that he was more tired than he'd expected. He showered, then lay down, meaning only to close his eyes for a few moments. But when he awoke five hours had passed and the sun was high in the sky.

He hurried downstairs and began to look for Norah. At last he heard the sound of her voice and followed it until he located the source behind a door that was slightly open. As he approached he could hear her saying, "I was pretty certain, but I wanted to be sure.... Thank you, you've eased my mind.... No, I don't think it would be good for the poor child to be snatched away like a piece of recovered property.... It's nice to know I can prevent it.... Don't worry, I can take care of Gavin Hunter. Bye." There was the sound of a receiver being replaced.

Gavin's mouth tightened. So that was her game. He'd actually tried to be nice to her, respecting her grief. And her reply was to kick him in the teeth. Right!

He pushed open the door and stood looking at her without speaking. She was sitting in a large office whose clutter filled his orderly soul with dismay. How did these people ever get anything done? She looked up and started slightly at the sight of him.

"I'll save time by admitting I heard the last part of your conversation," Gavin said grimly. "Let me make it clear that nothing you can do can keep me from my son. And if you really think you can 'take care of' me you've made a big mistake. Older and wiser heads than yours have made the same mistake, and regretted it."

"I'm sure you're very fearsome and terrible," she agreed, but without seeming overawed. "Peter certainly seemed to think so. Don't you realize that he heard what you said about removing him from me? He heard you shouting it in anger and it upset him almost as much as what happened last night."

"Nonsense. He's my son."

"Technically, but Tony was a father to him these past few years and he's forgotten any other home but this. If he wanted to go with you it would be different, but he doesn't, and so I won't allow it."

He almost smiled. "You won't allow it? *You* think you can tell me what you will and won't allow, when the issue is *my* son?"

"Yes, of course, he's *yours*, isn't he?" Norah said, a scathing note creeping into her voice. "Your property. I was forgetting. All right, let's fight this battle your way." She rose to confront him, and he had an odd sensation that she'd removed the gloves. "There can be more than one claimant to a piece of property."

"Not this one," Gavin said firmly.

"I've just been talking to Angus Philbeam, our lawyer. I wanted to check a point in Liz's will. Angus is a very thorough man. When he drew it up, he made Liz consider every possibility—even this one. Liz left the guardianship of Peter to Tony, and after him—me."

Gavin was silent for a split second before exploding, "You must be out of your mind!"

"You can visit Angus and see the will—"

"To hell with the will! No power on earth could give Liz the right to will my son's guardianship away from me. He's *mine.*"

Norah regarded him bitterly. "I'm beginning to understand why Liz always referred to you as Hunter," she said. "Not Gavin, but just 'Hunter.' She said you were so predatory that the name suited you perfectly."

"It makes a change from 'grating Gavin,'" he snapped.

"But she was right. You are predatory. Everything is prey to you—something to be fought for and snatched. And you win because you scare people. But I'm not scared. For one thing, even you wouldn't be inhuman enough to try to drag that child away today."

"I never said I was going to—"

"And for another you'll have to go through the courts to get Peter back, and I think they'll pay attention to that will. They'll pay even more attention to the fact that this is Peter's home, where he's been happy. He's just lost two parents—"

"*One* parent."

"And I don't think they'll let him be taken away from me by a father he hardly knows any more." The phone rang and she answered it quickly. She barely said a word, but whatever she heard seemed to please her because her face brightened. Finally she said, "I'll tell him at once. Thank you very much." She hung up and faced Gavin. "That was the Social Services. Angus has been on to them. They'll be sending someone to see you."

"Need I ask what this 'someone' is going to say? You seem confident that you have it all stitched up."

"They'll oppose any attempt to remove Peter from me so soon after the accident. He needs security, not another big change straight on top of the last one."

"And what kind of security can you offer him?"

"Love, and the stability of the home he's used to."

Gavin gritted his teeth. He hadn't meant to play rough, but she'd left him no choice. "But you're going to be leaving here. See what Social Services says when I tell them that."

"Leaving here? Why should I?"

"Look, I realize that your father was still a young man and you couldn't have dreamed that he'd die so soon."

"What does that have to do with what we're talking about?"

"It means that you have no right to stay in this house."

"Why?"

"Because it belonged to Liz—half of it. The other half is still mine. Liz's half will become Peter's and I—"

"Wait," she stopped him. "Liz didn't own any part of Strand House."

"I happen to know better. I bought this place originally and put it in our joint names, and the court awarded her half in the divorce settlement."

"Yes, I know all about that. What I'm saying is that Liz's share became Dad's some years ago, and he left it to me."

"*What?* That's impossible."

"It was to protect the sanctuary. He wanted to be sure that if anything happened to him I could carry on here."

"I don't believe what I'm hearing," he exploded.

But he did believe it. It had an awful inevitability. He'd always known that Tony Ackroyd had been a sponger who'd battened on Liz for her property. Now he discovered that he'd been a mercilessly efficient sponger. "You really do have this neatly arranged, don't you?" he said, breathing hard.

"I know you can't evict me, and for the moment you can't take Peter away from me. If you love your son, you won't even try to."

"Don't lecture me about loving my son," Gavin said dangerously.

"You frighten him—"

"That's impossible."

"I imagine anything's impossible to you, if it doesn't suit you. But Peter doesn't know you any more. Can't you understand that?"

"Yes, I'm beginning to. In fact I'm beginning to understand a good many things. You've turned his mind away from me, haven't you, and you think I can't take it back."

"You're right—I don't think you can *take* it back. You might *win* it back, but that's not your way, is it, Hunter? Your way is smash and grab, and it won't work this time."

"Oh, I have more weapons in my armory than you think. I can be patient and subtle when I have to be. You may be able to stop me removing Peter, but you can't keep me away from him. I have as much right to live in this house as you do, and that's what I mean to do."

"Live here? You mean to move in?" she echoed, dismayed.

"I've already moved in. So I'll be on hand to make sure my son isn't turned against me any more."

"But that's—" she sought for the word.

"Impossible?"

"Impractical. How can we live under the same roof?"

"It won't be for long," Gavin said. "Just as long as it takes you to realize that you can't defeat me. In the meantime, we'll just have to learn to endure each other."

Chapter Three

Mrs. Selena Bolden, a social worker, came the same day. She was middle-aged and hearty, with an uncomfortable likeness to a headmistress. As soon as she began to speak, Gavin's heart sank. Mrs. Bolden had known Liz and Tony well, liked them and had moreover been fed the story of how Gavin had tried to "kidnap" Peter six years ago.

"It would be most unfortunate if there were any similar, er, incident," she observed, looking at him closely.

Gavin controlled his temper and said calmly, "All I want to do is get to know my son again, so I'm going to live right here in my own house. At least you can't prevent me from doing that."

"Actually, I can," she said smugly. "I can apply for a court order preventing you from setting foot on these premises, and I could have one by this afternoon."

"*What?* My own house? Are you mad?"

"Whoever's house it is, the court would place the interests of the child first. Your previous attempt at kidnapping would be taken into account—"

"I keep telling you I did *not* try to kidnap my son—"

"Naturally you would say that, but the attempt is on the official record."

For the first time Gavin knew real fear. Everything he'd been so certain of was slipping away from him with terrible inevitability. Whatever the rights of the situation, it seemed that Norah Ackroyd had the power on her side, and he had no doubt she would use that power to thwart him.

But then, unbelievably, he heard her say, "Actually, Selena, I think Mr. Hunter is telling the truth." Gavin stared at her as she went on, "I saw what happened, and I don't think he would have really snatched Peter. Liz was hysterical and upset, and I believe she read too much into it."

Mrs. Bolden looked skeptical. "According to the official record," she said, like someone quoting the bible, "the little boy confirmed it."

"He confirmed that his father asked him to go with him, yes," Norah agreed. "But later he told me that Mr. Hunter had abandoned the idea when Peter made it clear he wanted to be with his mother. I tried to tell Liz, but she insisted I'd misunderstood. I know that I didn't."

"Are you saying you don't want me to get a court order?" Mrs. Bolden demanded, sounding disappointed.

"That's right. I don't. As you say, Peter's interests must come first, and right now none of us knows what's best for him. As far as I'm concerned, Mr. Hunter can stay here. I'll guarantee his behavior."

"Very well. I'll take your word for the moment." She eyed Gavin disapprovingly. "But no attempt must be made to remove Peter. Do I have your word on that?"

"Certainly," he said grimly.

Norah showed her out while Gavin tried to force himself to calm down. On the one hand he was possessed by sheer speechless outrage at Norah's impertinence at guaranteeing his behavior. But he knew that he owed everything to her generous intervention. In fact he owed her his total gratitude, and that was almost the worst thing of all.

When she returned he said with difficulty, "Thank you for speaking up for me. It wasn't what I expected."

"I never believed that kidnap story. You had ample chance to make off with Peter, but you didn't."

"But you could have had me thrown out of the house," he said bewildered. "Why pass up your advantage?"

He came from a world where only a fool let an opportunity slip, and this woman wasn't a fool. That was clear from the shrewd intelligence in her eyes as they surveyed him, their gleam showing that she fully understood his mystification.

"Maybe I was wrong to pass it up," she said. "We'll just have to see how things work out."

"I gave my word and I'll keep it. All I want is to rebuild my relationship with Peter."

"Well, I've given you the chance to do that," she pointed out.

"But I wish you'd tell me—why did you do it?"

"Because getting to know you again might be the best thing for him."

"I know that's what you told that woman but—"

She sighed. "Look, Hunter, the reason I gave was the true reason. I suppose in your sphere that's unheard of."

"Pretty well," he admitted.

"Well, welcome back to the real world."

"*Real* world? You call this—this Norah's Ark—the real world?"

"It's a sight more real than a businessman's fantasyland, where only figures on paper matter and the people they represent are treated as irrelevancies—or even nuisances."

Gavin took a deep breath. "I don't want to quarrel with you. You did me a favor, and I'm grateful. As you say, I have to get to know my son again, so if you don't mind I'm going to start now. Where is he?"

"Outside with the animals."

Gavin strode out of the house and through the grounds, confused by the profusion of large wire pens. He came across a woman mashing up feed. She was about sixty, very fat and puffing. Her grey hair was cut short and on her feet she wore a pair of ancient men's shoes. She eyed Gavin with a caution that revealed she'd been warned about him, but her manner was reasonably friendly. "I'm Iris," she told him. "I help Norah out with the animals."

He introduced himself politely and said, "I'm looking for Peter."

"He was here a moment ago, but he went off to do something else. Try down that path."

He followed her directions. As he pushed through a clump of hedges he could hear the sea in the distance, but there was no sign of Peter, just a young man in torn jeans and shirt, with his long hair held in a ponytail. He peered at Gavin from within a huge bird cage. A tall tree dominated the center of the cage and the young man was nearly at the top, making some repair, hanging by his knees like a trapeze artist. "Help you?" he called.

"Have you seen a boy of about ten?" Gavin called back.

"He came through here a while back, but he didn't stop. He was running to somewhere."

Gavin thanked him and went on. Another few yards brought him to the perimeter fence. He turned left and began to make his way back until he came to a large wire pen with a wooden hut at the rear. There was no sign of whichever animal lived here, but a scuffling inside the hut told him that there was an occupant. He was about to pass on when he heard more scuffling, followed by a soft, urgent, "Ssshh!"

He froze as the truth hit him. His son was hiding in that hut. But not from him, surely? Not from his own father?

"Peter," he called. *"Peter."*

He listened. There wasn't another sound, but despite the silence he knew Peter was in there. And now he had to face it. Peter was avoiding him. Tight-lipped, he stormed back to the house. "What in God's name have you told my son to make him run away from me?" he demanded when he found Norah.

"Nothing. You did it all yourself. I told you, he heard what you said about taking him away. You've got to reassure him about that before you can get anywhere."

"I was *trying* to reassure him. I wanted to tell him what we've agreed, that I'm staying here with him for a while."

"Well, he doesn't know that. He saw you barking at me, and that's the picture in his mind."

"I was angry because of Liz, because her death seems so senseless."

"I know." Norah looked at him with sudden sympathy. "I'm sorry," she said. "I didn't realize."

"Realize what?"

"That you still loved her," Norah said simply.

He stared at her, astounded. "Nonsense!"

"Is it? You were talking like someone who still felt awfully protective."

"Liz had that effect on people," he said awkwardly.

"I know." Norah gave a reflective half smile. "Dad was protective about her. So was I, in a way. She was so lovely and charming. It was wonderful having her as a mother. I hardly remember my real mother. I can't imagine anyone who'd ever loved Liz actually being able to stop."

"I stopped," he said firmly. "She betrayed me."

"And you turned your love off, just like that?" she asked skeptically.

He looked at her with hard eyes. "Is it any business of yours?"

"Not mine, but—it could be Peter's business. It might help him to know you still feel something for his mother."

"Unfortunately, I don't. Liz lost all power to hurt me on the day she walked out. And I don't see that it could make any difference to Peter one way or the other."

"I was thinking of the funeral."

"He won't be going to the funeral. It's no place for a child."

"That's for him to say. Of course I won't force him if he doesn't want to, but if he does want to it would be terribly cruel to keep him away."

"He's a child," Gavin said, aghast. "How can you even think of taking him into that grim atmosphere, letting him look at graves and coffins and—and people in black?"

"Gavin, it isn't funerals that are grim. It's death. And Peter is already facing death twice over. How he copes with it will depend on what happens now. People need the chance to say goodbye. If you deprive him of that chance, he'll feel it all his life."

He set his jaw. "I don't see it that way at all."

"Well, we'll let him decide."

There was a shadow in the doorway, and they both turned to see Peter standing there. He flinched when he saw his father and for a dreadful moment Gavin feared he would run away again, but Peter held his ground and looked at him silently. He looked strained and wretched, and Gavin's heart ached at the thought of what the child had to bear. "Why don't we go somewhere and talk?'' he asked, as gently as he could.

Peter didn't react at once. First he glanced at Norah for her agreement, and when she smiled he nodded at his father. Gavin's lips tightened. Could he have no communication with his own son except with her consent? But he held his tongue and left the room with Peter.

Once outside, father and son looked at each other awkwardly. ''Why don't you show me your room?'' Gavin said at last.

Obediently Peter turned and went upstairs, Gavin following. He had a large room with a view over the sanctuary. The walls were lined with pictures of birds and animals and charts showing creatures of the world. Gavin looked around him with displeasure. This wasn't what he thought of as a boy's room. Where were the football colors, the sports trophies?

''Now we can have some time alone together,'' he said more heartily than he felt. He made a gesture of half opening his arms that would have turned into a full embrace if Peter had responded. But the boy kept his distance and sat on the bed, watching his father warily. Gavin let his hands drop. ''You haven't said a word to me since I arrived,'' he said. ''That's no way to treat your father. What about, 'Hallo, Daddy?'''

He had the definite impression that Peter shrank back into himself. A small flame of anger flickered alight inside him. Was it a crime to want his son to call him Daddy? Or had that name been reserved for the other man, the enemy?

''I've looked forward to seeing you again,'' he persisted. ''I thought we could have a real father-and-son talk after all this time.''

Peter's silence seemed to mock the notion. The flame flared a little higher. ''We don't know each other as well as

I'd hoped," Gavin said, trying not to let himself feel the anger that he knew was kindling inside him. "But we'll have a chance now to—to—" inspiration failed him.

He began to stride about the room, trying to combat the hurt and disappointment that were like embers ready to be tossed onto the threatening fire, sending it out of control. "Did you put these things up?" he asked, looking around him at the pictures and charts. Peter nodded.

At that moment Gavin noticed something that seemed like an answer to a prayer. In the corner stood a small silver cup with something inscribed on it, the kind of sports trophy he himself had carried off as a schoolboy. Eagerly he seized it and read, *Presented to Peter Hunter, for outstanding work in school Nature Studies.*

He drew a sharp breath, too preoccupied with his own disappointment to notice that his son was watching him closely, with something in his eyes that might have been hope. "Is this the only one you've got?" he demanded. When he was answered by silence, he snapped, "For heaven's sake, answer me properly. I'm not going to eat you."

Instead of speaking, Peter opened a cupboard by his bed and took out a plaque which he handed to his father. It was a commendation from a bird-protection society. Gavin glanced at it briefly before looking away.

The bitterness was like bile in his throat. They had robbed him. His son was an alien to him. "That's all very well," he said in a constrained voice, "but haven't you got any manly interests? Don't you play football or cricket or—or something? Doesn't your school have teams?" The boy nodded. "Well, do you follow them? How do they do? Do they win matches?" He could hear his own voice rising as his desperation grew.

Peter considered this last question before answering it with a shrug. It might have meant no more than that sometimes the teams lost and sometimes they won. But to Gavin's lacerated sensibilities the shrug looked like contemptuous dismissal. "The sooner I get you away to a place where you can grow up properly, the better," he said furiously.

He was on the verge of shouting, and he knew he mustn't do that. So he vented his feelings by slamming down the little cup before saying, "We'll talk later—this isn't the right time," and striding out.

Gavin wasn't a man who gave up easily, but right now he was on the edge of despair. He knew he'd done every single thing the wrong way. And more frightening still, he didn't know what the right way was.

Left alone, Peter was motionless for a long moment. When he was sure Gavin wasn't coming back he went and lifted the cup whose stem had been bent by the force of his father's hand. He tried to straighten it, but after a while he gave up and put the crooked cup away in a drawer.

Gavin was an early riser. He was awake with the dawn next morning, and went down to the kitchen. A middle-aged woman with a severe face introduced herself as Mrs. Stone, the live-in 'help.' "I'm just starting breakfast," she said. "Can I pour you some coffee?"

"Later, thank you. I'm looking for Norah."

"She's out there, feeding those creatures."

The way Mrs. Stone sniffed and said, 'those creatures,' told Gavin he had a kindred spirit. "You don't care for them?" he asked.

"I wouldn't be here if jobs were easy to come by," she declared, sniffing again. "In my opinion animals should know their place, and it's not in the house. I made it clear when I took the job that I would have nothing to do with animals." Osbert honked from the floor. "Or birds," she added.

"Very wise," Gavin agreed with feeling. Through the window he could see Norah in the distance, talking to the pony-tailed young man who'd hailed from the birdcage. He hurried out.

She'd vanished by the time he arrived, but the young man was there. "Hi. I'm Grimsdyke," he said. "But everyone calls me Grim."

"Do you work here?" Gavin asked.

"I live here. I have a couple of rooms, and I pay my rent by helping out. If you're looking for Norah, she's gone to see Buster and Mack."

"Buster and Mack?"

"Buster's a donkey. Mack is his companion. Just go down that path and bear right."

Gavin followed the instructions and discovered Norah standing by a low wire fence, accompanied by Rex, the black-and-white dog that went everywhere with her. She was feeding mashed apple to an elderly donkey. "Good morning," she said pleasantly, but without taking her attention from the donkey. "Go on, eat it all up. Special treat."

"I take it this is Buster," he said, trying to match the distant cordiality of her tone.

"That's right. I got him two years ago from people who ought to have been shot. They'd neglected him so badly that his hooves had grown right under in curves and he could hardly walk. Would you believe they actually tried to prevent me removing him? I told them it was me or the law, take it or leave it. They took it."

"You always get your way, it seems?"

"Not always, but I'm a fighter."

"Is that a warning?"

"Take it how you like."

"Thanks."

They eyed each other appraisingly before Norah said, "I tried to find another home for Buster, but it didn't work out. He's very set in his ways."

"What does that mean?"

"Obstreperous."

"Then naturally he felt at home with you."

"Meaning we're two of a kind?"

"Take it how you like," he retorted coolly. "What about the other donkey? Did you have to shoot anyone to get him?"

"I don't have another donkey."

"Then who's Mack?"

She gave a soft whistle and a small monkey came bounding out of the trees, jumped onto Buster's back and from there into Norah's arms. "This is Mack," she said. "He's a macao monkey. Unfortunately they're very pretty."

"Why unfortunately?"

"It makes them popular as pets. They get bought by people who aren't fit to own a china monkey, let alone a live one." There was real anger in her voice.

The conversation wasn't going as he'd meant. He'd intended to greet her calmly, to be dignified and persuasive and make her see that she couldn't hope to claim half of Strand House. Instead he found himself discussing the sanctuary as if it were to be a permanent phenomenon. And it definitely wasn't. The thought reminded him of something else. "What's the idea of giving house room to that layabout?"

"If you mean Grim, I couldn't manage without him. And he isn't a layabout. Whatever he looks like, he's a brilliant zoologist. Unfortunately he's only here until he's finished writing his thesis. Then the university will give him a doctorate and research grant, and he'll vanish around the world."

"You relieve my mind. I was afraid it might be impossible to get him off the premises."

She swung around to face him. "You mean, your first thought was about the property?"

"That has to concern me. You've hardly improved the value of the property by—this." He made a gesture.

"That's all you see, isn't it, Hunter? Money, and how your financial position is affected. You judge everything by that yardstick, as though there were no other."

"It's as good a yardstick as any in a hard world," he declared grimly.

"Which is only another way of saying that you don't *believe* in any other yardstick." Her voice changed, grew softer, and curious. "Perhaps that's why you're so unhappy."

He was pale with anger. "Kindly leave my personal feelings out of this."

"I'm sorry. I didn't mean to get personal. It's just that when I sense sadness in anyone—human or animal—I just can't help…"

"Once and for all, I am not susceptible to whimsy."

She wore a puzzled frown. "I'm not being whimsical."

"This nonsense about sadness in animals! Animals are not sad, Miss Ackroyd."

"The ones who come here are."

"You know what I mean. They don't experience sadness in the way humans do."

"How do you know?"

"Because they are animals. They're not humans, they're *animals*. There's a difference."

"Actually, there's no difference. Surely you don't need me to tell you that human beings are animals?"

"Different kinds of animals," he said, knowing that he was unwise to be provoked into argument.

"Not different at all," she responded. "You'd be amazed how alike—"

"No, I wouldn't, because this conversation is going no further," he interrupted desperately.

"Yes," she said, regarding him and nodding as if she'd just been enlightened. "There are some things you find very hard to talk about, aren't there?"

"That's enough," he snapped. "If you think you can—"

He got no further. His speech was drowned out by a mad squawking, and the next moment a large white goose came half flying, half hopping toward them. He snapped at Gavin's legs, forcing him to back away hurriedly. The feeling of looking ridiculous increased his temper. "You'll get into trouble if you go around setting that vicious bird on people," he told her grimly.

"Osbert isn't a vicious bird," she protested.

He could hardly believe his ears. "Osbert?" he echoed outraged. "You call a goose Osbert? What are you running here? Disneyland?"

"You have a name, don't you?" she asked defensively.

"I'm not a goose," he snapped. "I'm a man. And my son is going to be a man. He's going to grow up in a man's world, seeing himself as a man—not Tarzan or Saint Francis, but a *man*. Do I make myself clear?"

"Perfectly. And now I'm going to make *myself* clear. I don't care about you or your half-baked prejudices, but I *do* care about Peter's feelings. He mustn't see us fighting. It upsets him too much, and I won't allow it."

"*You* won't allow—?"

"Do you have a problem with that?" Norah asked dangerously.

"I have a problem with you and everything about you, and I intend to resolve it my way. In the meantime, the best way for us to avoid quarreling is to avoid talking."

"That isn't practical. There are arrangements to be made. I'll consult you when I have to, but you can be sure it'll be as little as possible."

His gratitude for her intervention with the social worker had vanished without a trace. Now all he felt was the gall of being allowed to stay here by her consent, and the power she exercised over everything that should by rights be his—including his son. But she would just have to be endured while he bided his time. The important thing was to become a part of Peter's life again.

As he turned away from her he saw his son coming out of the house. He hurried toward him, but at a certain point Peter swerved suddenly sideways, so that his path and Gavin's didn't cross. Gavin stared, trying to believe it was an accident. There was still some distance between them, and Peter might simply not have seen him.

But in his heart he didn't believe it. Peter had turned aside to avoid him, and the pain was indescribable. After a moment he walked back to the house, taking care not to go in Peter's direction, and once inside he shut himself in his room.

Chapter Four

As the days passed and Peter still did not speak to him, Gavin faced the fact that his son had withdrawn into a silent world of his own. He eyed his father watchfully, suspiciously. If Gavin spoke to him he grew nervous and he would escape at the first possible moment. He seemed easier with Norah, but even with her he was silent. In fact the only creature with whom he now seemed at ease was Flick, the young fox who followed him around like a pet dog. Gavin had a terrible feeling of confronting a door that was bolted and barred against him. Somewhere—*somewhere*—there must be a key to his son's heart.

In desperation he called Mrs. James, the headmistress of Peter's school. She invited him to visit her and when he arrived she ushered him into her study with a friendly smile, but Gavin was morbidly conscious of the caution behind it. "How is Peter coping?" she asked as they sat down.

"It's hard to say," Gavin admitted. "He's become very withdrawn since his mother's death. I decided it would be best for him to stay at home for a while, especially since term is nearly over."

"Of course. In fact Norah had already informed me he wouldn't be returning this term," Mrs. James said, unaware that she was turning a knife in the wound. Norah had done this without consulting him. "But you told me on the phone that you wanted to know about your son's school progress."

"I haven't seen as much of him recently as I would have liked. Now I'm seeking any handle I can get."

"An excellent idea. I've got his marks out to show you. As you can see he's always in the top half of his class."

"How large is the class?" Gavin asked, glancing through the pages.

"Twenty."

He frowned. "Eigth or ninth. That's not very impressive."

"Does he have to impress you, Mr. Hunter?"

"I'd like to feel he was doing his best."

Mrs. Haynes hesitated a fraction before saying, "His overall marks may give a misleading impression. The fact is that there are times when he scores very high indeed. Then suddenly his work will plummet, and that pulls the average down."

Studying the pages again, he saw that she was right. Peter's marks went in peaks and troughs and he discovered, with a sinking feeling, that the troughs coincided with the times he'd visited his son. He made his face impassive. He didn't want this stranger to see the turmoil the thought caused him.

"Of course, marks only tell a small part of the story," she added. "Perhaps you'd like to look at his essays."

"Thank you." He began to look through the papers she offered him, hoping that there he could find some comfort. Mrs. Haynes went on talking kindly, trying to reassure him.

"As you can see, his grammar and spelling are excellent, and he can put his thoughts into words in a way that's quite impressive for a child of his age. You needn't worry about your son, Mr. Hunter. He's extremely bright."

He saw that, but he saw something else as well. All the ideas Peter couldn't express with his father he'd expressed on paper, and they were Tony Ackroyd's ideas. He emerged from his essays as a gentle, uncompetitive child, whose chosen companions were the animals amongst which he lived. One essay, called "My Favourite Kind of Day," described in detail how he was trying to train Flick. It was a charming piece of work, full of affection and cheeky humor.

Flick is a naughty fox who likes to do the opposite of what I say. So I tell her to do the opposite of what I really want. Sometimes it works, but sometimes she sees through it. She's very clever, so I have to be even cleverer. But when she does what I want, it's not because either of us is clever, but because we're friends. And friends are nice to each other.

But Gavin wasn't in the mood to appreciate the charm or the humor. All he could discern were the values of Tony Ackroyd and his daughter. In this and other essays, those values shone through every line. Bitterness possessed his heart as he realized this was yet more evidence that his son had been stolen from him.

"Thank you," he said, putting away the pages abruptly. "I've seen all I need to."

He made no further attempt to prevent Peter attending the funeral, and it became an accepted thing that the little boy was to go. For the next few days Gavin didn't seek out his son or try to be alone with him. He told himself that he was simply biding his time until the funeral was over, but the fact was he was afraid. He dreaded to see Peter running away from him, and dreaded even more the look of self-contained endurance that settled over the child's face when he encountered his father. He despised himself for his fear. It was a weakness. When faced with opposition, his way was to assert himself. But through his painful confusion he could just perceive that his best weapon was useless now. Assertion would only drive Peter farther away. So Gavin avoided it, but he didn't know what else to do.

He dreaded the funeral. His hostility toward both Liz and Tony, but mostly Liz, was mounting so intensely that he feared he might reveal it at an inappropriate moment. Norah's idea that he still loved Liz was outrageous, and her suggestion that he might show his feelings was typical of the unreality that, he felt, pervaded her whole life.

When the day arrived, he went through the first few hours as if in a dream. He'd done what was expected of him. A wreath, compiled of carefully anonymous flowers (no red roses: he'd made sure of that) had been delivered to the funeral parlor, with a card attached bearing the single name, Gavin. Now he was waiting, sober suited, for the funeral procession to arrive. He wished he could say something to Peter, who looked frighteningly pale and composed, but the words he might have chosen could only have been said between a father and son who were close. Now, more than ever, the gap between them yawned wide. And so no words were spoken.

The procession arrived. There were so many wreaths that each coffin had to travel in its own car. Gavin looked at the car that contained all that was left of Liz, hidden beneath a mountain of carefully composed flowers. "She'd have hated that," he said suddenly.

"Hated what?" Norah asked by his side.

"She hated flowers in formal arrangements. She liked to see them growing in the wild." Gavin couldn't have said why he suddenly remembered this, but it stood out in his mind, and with it came the memory of Liz as he'd first known her—young and free, her hair windswept. She had loved him in those days, but she'd turned into a sophisticated, elegant woman who'd run away from him. To what? To a man who'd given her the freedom to return to her true self? He would never know now.

He saw Norah looking about her, frowning. "What is it?"

"Peter. He was here just a moment ago, but he's vanished."

"Perhaps he doesn't want to go after all."

"Then he'd have let us know. He wouldn't just run away."

She ran back into the house, calling Peter, but there was no response. Gavin went out into the grounds and after a moment he saw Peter hurrying toward him. "What is it?" he asked. "Don't you want to go with us?"

The boy nodded. His eyes were wary and he seemed to be concealing something beneath the neat jacket he'd put on for the occasion.

Norah appeared. "Are you all right, Peter? Did you forget something?" He nodded, apparently to both questions. "Then let's be going."

They made the journey in silence. Peter and Norah, both pale and dry-eyed, sat close together and Gavin tried not to be too aware that they were holding hands, but he couldn't help knowing. His heart was bleak.

When they entered the chapel the two coffins were already in place, side by side. Norah laid her hand gently on Peter's shoulder to guide him into the pew, but he stopped suddenly. The two adults looked at him, concerned lest his composure should suddenly break, but Peter did something neither of them was prepared for. Lifting his head, he walked steadily toward his mother's coffin and reached into his jacket to draw out the thing he had been concealing there. It was a small posy of violets. Gavin had seen them growing wild on a bank by the sanctuary. He watched in wonder as his son carefully laid the wildflowers on top of a formal wreath, laid his hand on them for a moment, then stepped back. When he raised his eyes it was his father's face he sought, and Gavin's heart nearly stopped beating from joy. Slowly he smiled and nodded his head.

He felt a new happiness spread out and possess him. Peter had heard what he'd said about the wildflowers, and it had touched his heart. After all that had happened, there was still a faint spark of understanding between them. The knowledge softened him toward Liz. It was as if the hostile woman of the later years had vanished, leaving only the young, laughing girl he'd first loved, the girl who'd liked wildflowers. It was to that girl he spoke now in his heart.

I'm sorry, Liz. Whatever was my fault, I'm sorry. I hope you found happiness in the end.

He looked at the violets until, after a moment, they began to swim, as though he were seeing them through water. He rubbed his eyes and found to his surprise that they were wet. Something was hurting his throat.

He pulled himself together sharply, raising his head and swallowing hard. He didn't see his son looking up at him, nor the movement Peter made as if to slip his hand into his father's, then the cautious withdrawal, as if he'd thought better of it. But he was filled with happiness at the hint of understanding his son had given him.

And then it was all ruined. Just as Peter had held out hope, so it was Peter who smashed it by an innocently cruel gesture. The way out of the chapel led past the two coffins. Peter stopped for a moment, rested his hand on Tony's coffin and whispered, "Goodbye, Daddy."

Gavin felt his world disintegrate around him. The son who was too withdrawn to talk to him had managed to speak for Tony Ackroyd, had called him Daddy, the title Gavin regarded as his by right. He knew if he stayed here he would do or say something he would regret. Hardly conscious of his own actions or his surroundings, he pushed past his son and strode from the chapel. He walked hard and fast and didn't stop walking until he left the chapel far behind him.

His soul was in turmoil. He knew he'd done something shocking, but he couldn't risk pouring out his pain and bitterness before strangers. His own father's training in his childhood was still there. "Never let other people know what you're feeling—especially if you're feeling bad," William had said. "That kind of knowledge makes them strong and you weak."

And weakness was a sin. William had drummed that into him long ago. It was a sin he'd nearly committed just now, and he had to escape. He didn't look where he was going. He didn't care. He only wanted to get away as far as possible from Peter, from Strand House, from Norah who had witnessed his sickening defeat. How she must be rejoicing now in her triumph!

He walked and walked until every bone in his body ached. The light was fading fast and he was growing cold. Stopping, he looked around him and discovered that he'd come down to the shore. The tide was out, and he was walking along the flat, wet sands that stretched far out toward the horizon. All around him boats sat on the sand, lurching drunkenly to one side, waiting for the tide to come in and lift them afloat. Some people would have seen beauty and peace in the great empty shore. In his present mood Gavin saw only loneliness and desolation. In that moment it seemed to him that every single thing that mattered in his life had been taken away from him, leaving him naked and friendless. The business he'd built up was dying, the wife he'd once loved had gone finally, and his son—the one thing of value he might have salvaged from the wreck—his son was no longer his son. He was very close to despair.

He discovered that he was actually striding in the direction of the sea. Turning, he saw the land far behind him, a dark shadow in the fading light, and realized how far out he'd come. Heavy rain was beginning to fall, a wind was rising, and as he began to retrace his steps he found that his feet were wet. He wore a thin suit which gave little protection against the sudden damp chill. He began to run, but still it took him ten minutes to get to safety, and he could tell by the sound that the tide was coming in fast. He shivered and hurried back to the road.

Now he regretted coming so far without his car. He faced a good half hour's walk to Stand House, and he was shivering. He thought of the funeral reception that he'd missed, the way people would talk about him, and groaned. Worse, far worse, was what Peter would think. And Norah...

But he stopped there. Why should Norah's opinion matter? But it did. It shouldn't, but it did. He was too honest to deny the uncomfortable fact.

By the time he reached Strand House he was aching all over and it was nearly ten o'clock. There were few lights on and no cars in the drive, which meant that everyone had gone home. He let himself in quietly, thankful that the house seemed to be silent, and went to the drinks cabinet, where to his relief he found a full bottle of brandy.

Luck was with him and he didn't meet anybody as he climbed the stairs and went to his room. He took a hot shower, dried himself by putting on a toweling robe, poured himself a stiff measure of brandy, then another. He knew he should let someone know he was back, but first he must get warm. He poured himself another measure. Normally he drank very little, but tonight he needed help, and there was no other help to be found.

The brandy hit him like a punch in the stomach. Not only was he unused to spirits, but he'd eaten nothing at all that day. The thought of the funeral had destroyed his appetite in the morning, and a long walk on an empty stomach had left him vulnerable. To his relief the warmth began to steal through his veins, but it was only a warmth of the body. His spirit was still cold and despairing.

"You came back, then?"

He lifted his head and saw Norah standing in the doorway, dressed in pajamas. She was regarding him with cool hostility. "You had to go and do something spectacular," she said bitterly. "Never mind what it did to Peter. Never mind what it looked like."

"I couldn't stand it any longer," Gavin growled.

"Yes, that's what I told people. I spun a touching little tale of how your feelings overcame you, but I didn't tell them *what* feelings. I didn't say it was jealousy because Peter dared to call another man Daddy. I heard him, and I saw your face. You were ready to kill."

"Shut up," he said fiercely. "You don't know what you're talking about."

Norah came further into the room, shutting the door behind her. "Where have you been all this time?" He didn't answer but she noticed his clothes tossed over a chair and touched them. "You got soaking wet," she said.

The brandy was getting to him fast, turning logic on its head, confusing him, and at the same time simplifying all the kinks and subtleties of life. "I've been walking," he explained, "—on the beach—anywhere—I don't know." He added vaguely, "I think it's raining."

"You *think* it's raining?" she echoed, astonished. "It's a downpour out there."

"Then I expect that's why I'm soaking wet," he said, forming the words carefully.

"And disgustingly drunk," Norah observed.

"Yes," he conceded. "I'm disgustingly drunk, and I'm going to get disgustingly drunker. So clear out and let me get on with it."

Unexpectedly she sat down beside him on the bed. Her eyes no longer held condemnation, only surprised sympathy, as if she'd just understood something. "I'm sorry for what I said," she told him. "You weren't ready to kill at all, were you? More like ready to die."

He nodded and reached again for the bottle, but she stopped him. "No, don't do that. Talk to me instead. Dad always said talking to a friend was worth any amount of drinks."

"I don't have friends," he growled. "Just enemies and contacts."

"Well, aren't some of your contacts friends?"

"Not really. Even the best of them are deserting me fast."

She frowned. "Why?"

To his alarm he found he was on the verge of telling her everything, but he pulled himself together in time. "It doesn't matter."

"Anyway, I didn't really mean that. You need a shoulder to cry on right now."

"I don't have any of them, either," he said with a faint attempt at humor. "Isn't that what this is about?"

"I think this is about a man who only knows one way of showing his feelings, and that's to bawl and shout, and demand that people jump to it."

"Oh, really?" he said with tipsy gravity. "That's your considered opinion, is it, Miss Ackroyd?"

"Norah."

"Norah, who the devil are you to tell me what my problems are about?"

"Well, I may not be much, but right now I'm all you've got," she pointed out. "At least I'm here, and I'll listen."

"Ready to listen? Listen while I tell you everything you need to know to finish me off with that social worker?"

"Oh, stop that! We're not enemies this minute. We can't afford to be."

"Why's that?"

She sighed. "Because right this minute neither of us has anyone else to talk to."

He considered this and found it logical. "That's true." After a moment he added, "It's just as well we're not enemies tonight."

"Why tonight especially?"

"Because I'm disgustingly drunk," he reminded her.

"But you're not a drinker. I can tell. It's hit you like the first time."

"I'm not very used to it," he confessed. "To tell the truth, I hate the stuff. It's just that just now—I needed something."

"I know. Peter hurt you very badly, didn't he? But he didn't mean to. He's only a little boy, and a very unhappy one. He just said what he felt at the moment. You shouldn't expect him to calculate its effect on you."

"I don't. I don't want him to *calculate* anything. It's the fact that he feels that way that hur—that I mind."

"He's not the same child you used to know."

"I know," he said bitterly. "He's changed out of all recognition. Your father's doing."

"Nature's doing," Norah said firmly. "He's growing up. Don't blame Dad for that. You have to get to know Peter as he is now, not try to take him back to the past."

Gavin sighed. "I guess you're right. It's just hard after thinking about him after all these years, hoping we could get back together—then thinking I had the chance—and it all ends like this."

"But it hasn't ended," Norah said gently. "It's just begun. You have to give it time."

Time. The one thing he didn't have. He knew he should be in London this minute, fighting to recover what he could of his business. But he couldn't take away his son, and he couldn't leave him. To go now would be to give up hope.

Through the haze that covered his brain another thought made a brief appearance. "I really didn't try to kidnap him," he said.

"I know."

"But I *would* have, if he'd wanted to go with me. Only—he didn't."

He tried to say the last words casually. He didn't know that they came out sounding forlorn, so he didn't understand why Norah suddenly put her hand over his and squeezed. He froze, not knowing how to respond, and after a moment she withdrew her hand. "A child of that age needs his mother," she said. "The need for a father comes later, even with boys."

"And when Peter needed a father, someone else was there to scoop the pool," Gavin said wearily. His head was starting to ache.

"Scoop the pool? You make it sound like a lottery."

"Not a lottery. A treasure." Pain infused his voice. "You don't have children of your own, so you don't know how a child's love can be like finding a treasure. You don't know how you hoard it and relish it, and thank God for giving it to you, and hate anyone who tries to take it away."

"Gavin—" she said softly, but he didn't hear her.

"And even if you lose the child, you dream that you still have his love—"

"Of course you—"

"You go on dreaming even when everything seems against you. Because you believe, you see, in this mystical bond between yourself and your son that nothing in the world can break. And then you have a chance to get him back, and you picture how it will be—how he'll run to you crying, 'Daddy,' and you'll hug him and all the years apart will disappear." Gavin stopped and drew a shuddering breath. Norah was silent, regarding him with pitying eyes.

"But it isn't like that," Gavin went on at last. "He doesn't run to you. You're a stranger he won't even talk to, and some other man is Daddy. And there's nothing you can do about it."

He dropped his head into his hands. Norah watched him, appalled. It was in her nature to offer comfort to any hurt creature who came her way, but she knew this creature's wounds went too deep for words. She had an almost overwhelming desire to enfold him in her arms and heal him with the warmth of her body. She'd done that before, with troubled animals, holding them for hours, stroking and murmuring soft words until they fell asleep in her arms. It took all her strength not to reach out to Gavin now.

But he wasn't an animal. He was a prickly, complex man whom she knew would withdraw from her at any sign of pity. "No," she said at last, "there's nothing you can do about it except wait and let Peter come back to you in his own time. But if you rush it, you'll lose him. Like I said, it takes time, but—you're not very used to being patient, are you?''

"The things I've wanted have never been gained by patience. That's not the way to get anywhere in life."

"It's the only way with Peter. He's watching you all the time, waiting for the breakthrough, just as you are. Remember how he picked up what you said about the flowers?''

"Yes. It made me hope. That's a laugh."

"No, it isn't. Go on hoping. But remember that he's only a child and he's got a lot to cope with right now. Don't pile the emotional pressure onto him."

He stared at her vaguely. "Why are you telling me all this? We're on different sides."

"I'm on Peter's side. Aren't you?''

"Of course."

"Then we're not on different sides." She took the brandy bottle from him. "Don't drink any more of that stuff. Just go to bed and sleep it off." She touched the toweling robe. "This is wet."

"I put it on straight after a shower."

"The sooner you get it off, the better." She viewed him, seeming to realize for the first time that he was naked under the robe. "Put your pajamas on."

"You sound like a nanny," he complained.

"I feel like one. You need looking after, or you'll catch a chill after being out so long in the rain. Don't just lie down in that damp robe."

"All right." He drew the edges together. "I'll change after you've gone."

"Mind you do. Good night."

"Good night."

When she'd gone he closed his eyes, trying to find the strength to get up and change. His head was swimming, as well as aching, and his limbs had turned to lead, but he knew he mustn't fall asleep in the wet robe. He heard her voice saying, "Put your pajamas on." Interfering woman.

But she'd been kind and gentle, too, and that had soothed him. Like a nanny—or like a mother. His own mother had died too long ago for him to remember her clearly, but he was sure she'd cared for him like that.

But suppose it was no more than a trick to undermine him? Better be careful. Yet it hurt unaccountably to think badly of her.

He opened his eyes and closed them again at once. He would just lie down for a second, to give himself the strength to get up and change his clothes. The pillow was blessedly smooth under his cheek. It was only for a moment . . . just a moment . . .

He slept.

Chapter Five

Gavin awoke to a shocked recollection of everything that had passed the night before. The brandy had fuddled his mind then, but now the memory was devastatingly clear of how she had come into his room and held his hand and lured him into lowering his guard.

Perhaps she hadn't deliberately lured him, he thought, trying to be fair. Perhaps he'd done it himself, but the result was the same. He'd allowed her to see past the armor of reticence that was his only defense and discover his weakness. Whatever her apparent sympathy, at heart they were still opponents, and he'd yielded to her spell like a heartsick boy. Shivers of shame went through him.

Throwing back the covers he discovered something that appalled him still further. He was wearing his pajamas. Searching his mind frantically, he was unable to recall putting them on. His last memory was of lying down on top of the bed in the damp robe. But the robe had now vanished.

A search revealed it on a hanger behind the bathroom door. Norah must have returned, gone through his dresser to find his night wear, stripped the robe off him and somehow managed to get the pajamas on. And he'd been drunk enough to sleep through it all.

He knew he should be grateful. He took cold easily, and if he'd slept in the wet robe he would have developed a nasty chill. But for the moment all he could think of was the sheer effrontery of the woman who had dared to strip him naked while he was unaware. The fact that it was his own fault only made her crime more unforgivable.

As he dressed he reflected that it wasn't too late. When he looked into her eyes the consciousness would be there, but if he kept the consciousness out of his own eyes it would die in hers. What he didn't remember couldn't be used against him.

He had a moment's distress at what he was going to do. The memory of feminine warmth and kindness was so alluring that he was almost tempted to yield to it. But that was exactly what she wanted him to do. He must never forget that such thoughts were dangerous, never forget to be on his guard against her.

But with all his heart he wished it weren't necessary.

Norah came into the house from her early morning rounds of the animals. Peter had been out with her, conscientiously performing all his tasks. He'd long ago absorbed the only discipline that counted in the sanctuary, that the care of the animals came first. Your heart might be broken, you might be dying inside, but the helpless creatures who depended on you still had to be fed and cared for. It had given him a maturity well beyond his ten years, and she guessed that at this moment it gave him strength.

She could only guess, because even with her he was silent, although he would sometimes press close to her. In the last few days the only time she'd heard him speak had been when he whispered, "Goodbye, Daddy" in the chapel. And when Gavin had pushed past them and stridden out of the chapel, Peter had turned his gaze up to her as if seeking reassurance. She'd hated Gavin at that moment, and she'd hated him even more when he didn't come back for the rest of the day. She'd gone to his room still hating him, but there she'd found a drenched, desperate man who'd turned to the bottle to assuage his pain. The fact that he couldn't cope with the brandy had been a gleam of vulnerability that had helped soften her.

She'd found herself forgetting their enmity and striving to comfort him. He'd called her a nanny, and she'd agreed. It had been the instinct that had made her return later to make sure he was all right, only to discover him asleep on top of the bed, still wearing the damp robe. She'd tried to awaken him, but he'd been very deeply asleep, and at last she'd taken action, finding his pajamas and maneuvering him into them. It had been difficult to cope with his deadweight, but not as difficult as she'd feared. She was strong and there was muscle but no fat on his long bones, and the feel of his flesh had been firm and smooth against her hands.

The memory of that came back to her now, along with the sight of his smooth chest and lean hips, and suddenly she felt her whole body suffused with warmth. The sensation took her by surprise. She lived so close to nature that physical embarrassment was almost unknown to her, and for a moment she wondered what was happening. Then she remembered how he'd fallen against her while she was putting on his jacket, how his head had rested against her breasts, and how sweet the feeling had been.

She made herself coffee and was sitting in the kitchen sipping it when the sound of Gavin's footsteps made her jump. She looked up as he came in, but the smile died on her face as she saw the chilly distance in his eyes. "Good morning," he said distantly.

"Good morning," she said, watching him.

"I'm sorry about yesterday. I shouldn't have walked out of the funeral like that, but..." he shrugged, "things got a bit much for me. Did it cause much trouble at the reception?"

"No, I...explained that you'd been under a lot of strain." Norah spoke slowly as it dawned on her that they'd covered the same ground last night.

"Thank you. I suppose I should tell you where I went."

"There's no need," she said significantly.

"You're entitled to an explanation," he said coolly. "I took a long walk to clear my head. I went down to the shore and walked out in the direction of the sea. By the time I came back it was pouring with rain and I got soaked. I should have told you I was back, but I didn't want to risk taking cold, so I went straight to bed."

Norah took a deep breath before making her voice carefully neutral. "That's perfectly all right. I hope you're all right this morning."

"Fine, thank you. Can you tell me where Peter is? I should say something to him."

"What are you going to say?" she asked quietly.

"I'm going to apologize to him, of course. What happened wasn't his fault."

"I'm glad you realize that."

He looked at her angrily. "Credit me with some understanding. He's only a little boy, and a very unhappy one. I'm not going to pile a lot of emotional pressure on him..." he checked himself, drew a swift breath, and walked out. Norah stared after him, astounded at hearing her own words quoted back to her, and wondered how much, if anything, Gavin really remembered about last night.

Gavin found his son feeding Buster and Mack. He approached him slowly and with caution. He seemed to have stripped away an outer skin this morning, and to have a new sensitivity. It told him now that Peter was conscious of him long before he seemed to be, and full of tension. At last the child looked up. "Are you all right?" Gavin asked.

Peter nodded.

"I'm sorry about the way I left yesterday. I shouldn't have done it but—we all do things we shouldn't, at some time." Peter nodded, and Gavin was emboldened to go on. "I found myself remembering your mother as she was years ago, before things were bad between us. That's how you should always remember people when they die." Peter nodded again, and this time he also managed a faint smile. Relief flooded Gavin. It was communication of a sort.

Peter had finished his work. He left the pen, shutting it carefully behind him, then took a few steps away, looking back over his shoulder as if indicating his father should follow him. Gavin did so, and Peter led him almost to the edge of the sanctuary and pointed at a bank where wild violets made a show of color among the green. As he met his son's gaze Gavin understood why he had been brought here, and he knew more relief, tinged with happiness. "Yes," he said. "This is where you got the flowers yesterday, wasn't it?" The child nodded. "I'm glad. She would have liked that so much."

This time there was no doubt about it. Peter actually smiled. It was only a brief smile before he became once again the withdrawn child he usually was, but it had happened. Gavin's conscience pricked him. He knew the debt he owed Norah for this moment. In justice he ought to acknowledge it, even thank her. But that would be another demonstration of weakness to add to last night, and he couldn't quite make himself risk it. Besides, it was probably just part of her cleverness, and he ought to be more wary of her than ever.

The following day he received an unwelcome phone call. "Hallo, Father," he said reluctantly.

Despite William's ailment, his voice sounded loud and forceful in Gavin's ear. "Got the funeral over with yet?" William demanded, coming straight to the point. Gavin couldn't remember a time when his father had wasted his energy over people's sensibilities.

"The funeral was yesterday," he said.

"When's that woman leaving?"

"All in good time. I can't just throw her out."

"Why not?"

"For one thing she owns half the place."

"Rubbish. Legal technicality. A good lawyer will drive a coach and horses through it. Get rid of her and start raising your son properly. I've had some ideas about that. Bring him to see me as soon as you can and we'll talk. I'd like to see if your boy is turning into a real Hunter."

"He's Liz's boy as well," Gavin reminded him.

William snorted. "Yes, and look what she did with him. Brought him up a namby-pamby, I shouldn't wonder."

This had been Gavin's own thought, but he immediately said, "You're prejudging the situation. Peter may be only a child, but he already seems to me to be a—a strong person."

"Let's hope you're right. The world belongs to the strong. I hope you've told him that."

"I've told him what I think is appropriate," Gavin said in a tight voice, "but his mother was only buried yesterday and—"

"All right, all right," William interrupted him, evidently uninterested in any point of view other than his own. "While you're wasting your time down there, who's minding the store?"

"My assistant, Miss Fuller. She's coming down here soon, and we'll work from Strand House."

"Huh! Women!"

"She happens to be excellent at her job."

"If you say so. Look here, I've written you a long letter, giving you my views. You'll get it tomorrow. Just take what you need and discard the rest. You know I never interfere."

Gavin grunted and hung up as quickly as he decently could. He dreaded William's bouts of 'not interfering.'

The letter arrived next morning and proved to be so prejudiced and ignorant that Gavin couldn't finish it in one sitting. He put it away, then called his office to make final arrangement for Miss Fuller's arrival. But she wasn't in yet, which was unlike her.

He was running short of cash, and he decided to go into the nearest town to find a bank. When he'd finished there, he called his office again from a pay phone. But Miss Fuller still wasn't there and nobody seemed to know where she might be.

He bought a local paper and went into a café, hoping to finish the letter in what he hoped would be peace and quiet, but he found himself getting more agitated as he read. Every line, every word, proclaimed the rigidity of William's mind, and the utter impossibility of broadening his horizons. This had always been true, but now it seemed to strike Gavin with new force.

For a moment he wondered how life would be if William were a man of sensitivity and understanding, a man a son could talk to when he was in trouble. But the thought was self-contradictory. Sensitivity and understanding had no place in William's scale of values, and strong men were never "in trouble" according to him. In fact there was only one person Gavin could confide in and receive sympathy from, and she was off-limits.

He put the letter away and opened the local paper. There was a description of the funeral of "naturalist and local celebrity Tony Ackroyd," plus a few quotes from Norah about the sanctuary. Gavin glanced through them and was about to close the paper when he came to one phrase that stood out as if written in neon. He drew a sharp, angry breath, drained his tea and hurried out to his car.

As soon as he arrived home he went in search of Norah and found her in her on-site office. There was no sign of Peter. He was glad of that. He needed space to fight. "What the devil did you mean by this?" he demanded, pushing the paper in front of her.

She read the item and smiled. "They've done them proud, haven't they? Tony and Liz were always very popular around here."

"That's not what I meant. What right did you have to tell this paper that in future the sanctuary was going to be called Norah's Ark?"

"I think it's rather a nice name."

"Nice? You know my opinion of whimsy."

"Well, you shouldn't have suggested it if you didn't want me to use it."

"*I* suggested it? Are you mad?"

"I admit you said it pretty scathingly. In fact you said 'this Norah's Ark of yours,' as though you were holding it away from you with tongs. But I thought it was a good name, just the same."

"So you appropriated it," he seethed.

"Well, you didn't want it for yourself, did you?"

"I—that is not the point."

"What *is* the point?"

"The point is that you're quoted here as saying that the name was suggested by a generous well-wisher. And you can have no illusions about how badly I fit that description."

She looked at him wryly. "Neither generous nor a well-wisher, huh? No, I suppose not. But before you go letting off steam about it, I should tell you that Peter loves the idea. And he was thrilled when I told him it came from you."

Gavin struggled to control himself. "You are the most unscrupulous woman it's ever been my misfortune to meet."

Instead of coming back to him Norah looked suddenly weary, as though she'd been keeping up a brave front that had become too much. "Look, Hunter," she sighed, "it wasn't an evil conspiracy. I just happened to mention it to the reporter and he said what a wonderful name to call the place in future, and I said, yes, wasn't it? It just slipped out. I won't use it if you really hate it."

Oh, she was clever, he realized offering to backtrack after getting Peter keen. And who'd get the blame for that?

"If Peter likes it, you have to use it," he said grimly.

She fired up. "Don't tell me what I have to do."

"I *am* telling you. I'm not going to let you blacken me to my son by telling him I vetoed it."

"But you—"

"Norah, you will call this place Norah's Ark, and that's an end of the matter."

She gritted her teeth. "Yes, Hunter," she said in exasperation.

He left the office abruptly and strode towards the house, but as he reached it he heard her running after him. "By the way," she said as they went inside, "there's been a delivery for you. Several boxes of files." She indicated a huge pile of boxes standing in the hall. "They were delivered by a Miss Fuller."

"She's my secretary and personal assistant," Gavin said. "Where is she now?"

"She's gone."

"What do you mean, gone?"

"I mean gone, as in 'gone away,' 'left the premises,' departed in her big, shiny car without a backward glance at us dumb yokels."

"But why? She was supposed to move in here, to work with me." His eyes narrowed as the asperity in her last remark got through to him. "Did you make her leave? Because if you did, let me tell you that I consider that an unpardonable intrusion into my—"

"It had nothing to do with me," Norah interrupted. "From the way she looked around, I think she's a city lady who considers this the back of beyond. Anyway, she must have made her decision before she came here, because she had this all ready for you."

She handed him a sealed envelope. Gavin tore open the letter and discovered a neat, impersonal communication from the efficient Miss Fuller, in which she informed him that she'd found another job and was leaving immediately.

Something clutched Gavin's stomach as he read it. He had no particular fondness of Miss Fuller, but he knew she had an admirable nose where the financial markets were concerned. Her departure at this moment meant only one thing. She didn't believe he was going to pull Hunter & Son out of its present mess, and she was voting with her feet. It was a sharp reminder that he had other problems in addition to Peter, problems he'd been neglecting lately.

"Trouble?" Norah asked in a sympathetic tone.

"None that I can't cope with," he said cheerfully, slipping the polished mask into place as so often before. "As you guessed, she likes the bright lights. This wouldn't suit her at all. But I can manage without her for a while."

She looked at him. "Are you sure that's all it is?"

"Perfectly sure," he said in a tone that snubbed her. "Now, I have to find somewhere to work. I seem to remember there's a desk available in the office."

"Well, yes, but—" it was clear she didn't want him in what had been her father's office.

"There's an extra telephone plug in there for a fax machine," he pointed out. "I saw it. Also plenty of outlets and shelves. It's the logical place."

"True, but—"

"And since you work there as well, we can answer the phone for each other," he finished smoothly.

"Hmm! I wonder who'll end up taking the most messages for whom?" she asked shrewdly.

"Meaning?"

"Meaning that you'll try to use me as an unpaid secretary."

"I can't think why you say that—"

"Because I see right through you, Hunter. I know the kind of man you are. A user. All right, you can move into the office, but you make your own coffee, answer your own phone and do your own filing."

"I'm innocence personified," he assured her.

"Hmm!"

He'd believed his own declaration of innocence at the moment he made it, but he hadn't realized how used he was to having Miss Fuller as backup. It was natural to him to say,

"Put that file away for me," or "Get me so-and-so on the phone," and he went on doing it. But only for a while. Norah would invariably remember something she had to do outside, and he would find himself talking to thin air.

Sometimes the phone would ring and he would snatch it up, growling "Hunter," only to find himself talking to someone who wanted Norah. Then he would have to drop his own work and go in search of her, which was exasperating. To cap it all, when challenged, Norah seemed incapable of understanding that it was an intolerable intrusion for a busy man like himself.

"This is the last time I'm doing this," he said when he'd hunted her down in the sanctuary and thrust a message into her hand. "I had to waste valuable time placating that man because you'd said you'd call him back and then you didn't."

Norah glanced at the name on the paper. "I didn't call him back because you were hogging the phone yesterday," she said crossly. "You might have noticed—except that you never notice anyone else's concerns—that I kept looking in hopefully, but you never once let go of the receiver. That's why I didn't call him back, and if you had to calm him down you got your just deserts. That's all I have to say."

"If only it were. The phone is part of my business—"

"Then get one of your own and stop hogging mine. I have business to deal with, too, and you're holding it up."

"Oh, come on," he scoffed.

"And what does 'come on' mean?" she asked dangerously.

"It means there's business and business. There's my business—property—"

"And money," she reminded him ironically. "Don't forget money."

"And money," he agreed. "Money and property. Things that are real. Surely you don't expect me to believe that a few donkeys matter in comparison?"

For a moment he thought she would explode, she was so angry. But she calmed down enough to say, "You don't deal in things that are real, Hunter. You deal with lights on a computer. Turn a switch and the whole lot disappears. There's no reality in that. Try cleaning out a pen when an animal's living in it. That's reality, and no convenient switch to make it vanish."

"That's hardly—"

"Be quiet, I haven't finished. You say, what do a few donkeys matter? Ask your son if they matter, if he'll answer you. They matter to him, because he's unhappy and they're keeping him sane. They're his lifeline—and mine. Put your arms around an animal, feel its warmth, and feel your own warmth flowing in response. That's not only reality, it's healing. Warmth and love are the most healing things ever created, and nobody ever healed anything by signing checks."

He opened his mouth, but she charged on over him. "Do you know who this man is?" she asked. "He runs a school for damaged children. Some of them are physically disabled, and some are sick in their hearts and minds. I've promised him he can bring a group of them here, and I've been trying to call him to fix the date. Now I'm going to call him back and apologize for keeping him waiting, but your bricks and mortar, your bits of paper and your computer lights are more important than his sick children. Would that be putting it fairly, do you think?"

"I think it's damned *un*fair," he burst out. "But you're very clever at twisting things to suit your own argument."

"Well, I have to keep my wits about me with you," she flashed back.

"I don't know why you're so ill tempered, just because I came to give you a message," Gavin said, retreating into dignity.

Norah didn't know, either. The strength that had sustained her in the early days after the tragedy seemed to be seeping away now. At the same time her burdens grew heavier and every day seemed filled with clouds, even when the sun was out. It took only a small thing to make her fly off the handle, as she'd just done.

"You didn't just come to give me a message," she said. "You came to complain about *having* to give me a message. Now that you've delivered it, we have nothing further to say."

She headed back to the house, leaving Gavin watching her and reflecting what an impossible woman she was.

His activities grew more frantic as the skies over Hunter & Son darkened. It was madness to remain here. He should be in London, wheeling and dealing, challenging rivals to see who would blink first. But now there were no such confrontations because he was doing everything from a distance. And he was losing by it.

It soon became clear that Miss Fuller's defection had soon passed along the grapevine. Contacts telephoned, full of barely concealed curiosity. They murmured agreement when Gavin explained that Miss Fuller preferred the city, but they knew the truth. Gavin could hear the line humming with their unspoken knowledge.

"Why don't you go and see some of these people?" Norah demanded, exasperated.

"Sure, you'd just love me to go, wouldn't you?" he asked coolly. His nerves were in shreds. "And what would I find when I came back? The locks changed, I shouldn't wonder."

Norah pushed back a lock of untidy hair and looked at him with weary distaste. "If I had the energy I'd throw something at you for saying that," she observed.

"Remind me to duck sometime."

"You can laugh, but my aim is perfect—as I'm sure you'll discover one day. Luckily for you I'm dead beat."

She collapsed in a leather armchair, with her legs over the side. She was dressed in a pair of old shorts that looked as if they'd been cut down from jeans, topped off by a small sleeveless vest. The outfit had clearly been chosen for comfort and convenience. It was impossible to imagine this hostile young woman wanting to appear seductive to him. Yet he was disturbingly conscious of her long, bare legs, the beauty of her neck, the way her breasts swelled against the thin vest, and the rosiness of her skin that looked as if it smelled of the sun and the wind.

"Of course the locks won't be changed," she told him. "We'll all still be here when you get back."

He regarded her suspiciously. "Really?"

"Well you can bring a pickax to knock down the door if I'm lying, can't you?" she demanded, exasperated. "For heaven's sake, Hunter, go. Give us a rest from each other. We'll both benefit."

"You mean Peter will benefit?" he snapped.

"Actually, I was thinking of myself," she snapped back.

"Fine. Then I'll spend tomorrow in London."

"Do that. Spend the day after, too, and the day after that—"

"Just tomorrow. You don't get rid of me that easily."

She grinned at him cheekily. "Shame!"

Chapter Six

He was gone three days, and managed to fix up some short-term finance that would give him a breathing space, though it would also increase his debt. On the last evening he went to have dinner at the home of Brian Kendel, a business contact with whom he was vaguely friendly. He found his host and hostess a little flustered and behind with their preparations. "We started playing with the new toy and forgot the time," Brian said self-consciously.

"New toy?" Gavin echoed politely. He had visions of an executive knickknack, all clicking beads and colored lights, such as were supposed to relieve stress in businessmen.

But his host produced a neat little camcorder. "It's our second," he explained. "We got the first one when Simon was born, three years ago. Now that we've got Joan, as well, we bought a new one. When the kids are grown-up we can rerun the tapes. It's like snapshots, only better."

He played a tape on the television, showing his baby son from the first day to his third birthday. Gavin watched with a fixed attention that was more than mere politeness and made his hosts think well of him. In fact he was merely thunderstruck by the realization of how much of Peter's growing he'd missed, and the discovery of how he could at least fix the present on tape.

"Where can I get one of these things?" he asked urgently.

He left London next day with the latest model on the backseat of the car. All the way to Norfolk he was thinking of the pleasures of using it. Perhaps Peter would be intrigued by the machine, they could discover its workings together, and at last break through the barrier that still separated them.

The road home took him along the coast. The tide was still out, although coming in fast, and he looked across the flat sands where the boats were just beginning to float again, remembering the time he'd been here, and all that had happened that night.

He slowed the car as he saw two figures, one tall, one short, walking out in the direction of the sea. Even at this distance he was sure they were Norah and Peter. In his present mood, he felt charitable toward all the world. He would follow, and show them the camera and the three of them could enjoy it together. He stopped the car and called to them, but they were too far out to hear. Gavin began to run after them.

Peter was carrying a box, which he put carefully down on the sand and opened. The two of them were so absorbed that they weren't aware of Gavin, although he was now quite close. He heard Norah said, "Lift him out." Peter reached into the box and took out a sea gull, which he held carefully between his two hands.

He set the bird down on the sand and took a step back. There was something natural and practiced about his movements, as though he'd done this many times before. The sea gull hesitated a moment before pattering a few tentative steps. Then it seemed to smell the salty air and sense the breeze on its back. It moved faster—then faster—and suddenly it was airborne, winging away across the water, directly into the sun. Norah and Peter watched it go, their hands shading their eyes.

But suddenly Peter brought up his other hand to cover his face and turned so that he could hide against Norah. She embraced him at once. "I loved Joey, too," she said. "But it's better for him to fly back to his natural life. He'll be happier that way."

But Peter shook his head violently and cried in a muffled voice, "It's not *Joey*."

Norah sighed and held him more closely. "I know. Mum and Dad. They used to love releasing things back to the wild, and we're going to remember them every time we do this. But, darling, one day it won't hurt. It'll be like the gull. We'll remember only the time we had together and be grateful for it, and we'll understand why we had to say goodbye. That time will come. I promise."

Pain slashed through Gavin. It was akin to the pain he'd felt at the funeral when Peter had whispered "Goodbye, Daddy." But that had only been a moment. This seemed to last for an age. Gavin regarded himself as a man in control of his emotions, but this was more than he could cope with. His misery gave birth to a cruel demon, and it was the demon that spoke harshly from within him, saying, "And the sooner it comes, the better."

They whirled and stared at him. There was shock and dismay in Peter's face, horror in Norah's. "For pity's sake!" she said angrily. "Do you have to—?"

"Yes, I have to, because I'm tired of this. I've been patient while you turned my son into a namby-pamby, but I won't allow it any longer. At some point he's got to grow up and stop crying."

Peter wrenched himself away from Norah. If he'd run to his father Gavin would have opened his arms to him, but Peter avoided him and fled back across the sands in the direction of home. Gavin turned to go after him, but Norah seized his arm.

"To think I believed you were learning a little sensitivity," she raged. "It was all a front, wasn't it? The truth is that you're harsh and cruel and completely without understanding. You don't care for Peter as a person. If you did, you couldn't have acted like that. He's a possession you came here to reclaim, and you're getting impatient with having to go slowly."

"If you mean that Peter is mine, you're right—"

"You saw Liz in the same way. That's why you lost her. You think about nothing but possessions, money and success."

"Success matters. That's how a man knows what he is."

"Well, what are you?" she demanded. "A man whom nobody loves."

He hardened his face, refusing to let her see that this accusation was like a blow to the stomach. "There's more to life than love," he grated. "I want my son brought up to see things as they are, not through the rose-colored spectacles you all wear in this place."

"What do you mean, rose colored?"

"I mean today's touching little ceremony. Sick creatures don't always recover, and there isn't always a happy ending. You call me harsh. Well, life *is* harsh, and he'll survive better if he's prepared for it."

"Don't you think he already knows life is harsh?" she cried. "He just lost two people he loved."

"He still has his father, and eventually you'll have to let him come with me. If you're sensible, you'll face the inevitable now."

"I don't believe it *is* the inevitable. I won't lose hope. Liz used to say I had a touch of Mr. Micawber in me, and she was right. I always believe something will turn up."

"And just what kind of miracle do you think is going to turn up?" Gavin asked skeptically.

"Anything might happen. The court might decide that Peter belongs with me, where he's happy. Or you might decide the same thing."

"That will never happen," he snapped.

He turned on his heel and went back to the car. When he reached Strand House he went in search of Peter. He found him making up feed with Grim, the two of them working quietly together, anticipating each other's movements. It was clear they'd done this often before. It was Grim who looked up and saw Gavin, but he was sure Peter had known he was there and simply refused to acknowledge him. "Looks like you're wanted," Grim said.

Reluctantly, it seemed to Gavin, Peter lifted his head. His eyes were distant. "I'd like to talk to you," Gavin said.

It was unnerving the way a child could be so docile, while still shutting out his father. He set down what he was doing and came toward Gavin, but there was no communication in his manner. His obedience was simply another form of armor.

"Look, I know you think I was hard on you just now," Gavin said awkwardly. "Perhaps I was. Harder than I meant to be. It's this place. I'm not comfortable here, and it makes everything wrong between us. We can't get to know each other properly."

Peter's lips didn't move, but his eyes said, "Why not?"

"Because we can't talk proper...I mean, I need to be able to talk to you without feeling you're going to run off to Norah as soon as I've finished. She's a fine person but—we're father and son. We may not have seen much of each other, but we're still father and son. We always will be. Nothing can ever change that." Perhaps he said the last words a little too firmly.

Flick appeared from nowhere and brushed against Peter's leg. The boy reached down and scratched her red coat absently. "You might look at me while I'm talking to you," Gavin said tensely, and Peter straightened up at once. But his very obedience seemed like a kind of snub. It was as if he were saying, "I'll obey you in every detail, to cover the fact that my heart isn't with you."

Gavin felt a snub keenly, and despite his good intentions it put an edge on his voice. "This place is nothing but a fool's paradise, and nobody ever gained anything from living in a fool's paradise. You've got to learn how to fight the world like a man, and you'll only learn that with me."

As soon as the words were out of his mouth, he had an eerie feeling—as if the world had sideslipped. The air seemed to sing about his ears. It was as if he were living this moment for the second time, and the first time was there with him, still living, endlessly repeating. He gave himself a little shake. It was the first time he'd ever experienced a sensation of déjà vu, and it baffled him.

"Do you understand what I'm saying?" he demanded. "I don't want my son to be a milksop, and that's what you'll be if you stay here."

Unexpectedly Peter turned and looked at him with a look Gavin had never seen before. For the first time his eyes weren't distant and withdrawn, but angry and defiant. "Don't look at me like that," Gavin shouted. As Peter began to turn away, something snapped within him. "Don't turn away from me. I'm talking to you." He seized his son by the shoulders and forcibly swung him round, shaking him slightly. "Don't," he shouted. "Don't do that. I'm your father. Why can't you..."

He didn't finish the sentence. He didn't really know what he was trying to say. He had an overwhelming impulse to pull the child against him and enfold him in a gigantic hug, but a self-control perfected too long ago to remember restrained him.

"All right," he said with a sigh. "I'm sorry. Run along now."

He turned sharply and walked away. If he'd looked back he might have seen his son watching him with a longing expression that would have given him hope. But he didn't look back.

That evening at sunset Norah walked down near the shore. She could hear the waves splashing as the tide, which had come in, began to withdraw. She walked until she saw Gavin sitting on a rock staring out over the water. "You weren't there for supper," she said.

"I didn't want any."

"If it's any interest to you, Peter's very unhappy."

"Of course it interests me, but he doesn't want my comfort. If I reach out to him, he runs away. You know that."

"Perhaps that's because when you reach, you grab. You might get further by waiting for him to come to you."

"I could wait forever for that," he said bitterly.

"Well, what do you gain by sitting out here sulking."

"I'm not sulking. I came back to get my camcorder, but of course it was too late."

She sat down beside him. "What camcorder?"

"I bought one in London. I wanted to film Peter. I've missed so much of his growing up, and I thought I could catch him now. I brought it down the beach this afternoon. I was going to show it to both of you. But I must have dropped it somewhere."

"Well, you can always get another."

He shrugged. "What's the point? He'll probably hate the idea, anyway."

She considered this. "If you just point the camera at him he probably will hate it," she agreed. "Little boys don't like being photographed or filmed. It embarrasses them. Didn't you try to get out of it when you were a child and your father wanted to take snaps of you?"

He gave a mirthless laugh. "He never wanted to. He'd have called it a sentimental waste of time."

"And your mother?"

"I can barely remember her."

Norah nodded, as if she'd understood something. "If you want to film Peter, why don't you tell him it's Flick you're interested in?" she said.

"How would that help?"

She sighed. "Hunter, sometimes you can be painfully slow. You ask Peter to hold Flick up for the camera, then Peter's so busy thinking of Flick that he forgets you're filming him, too. That way he won't be self-conscious and you'll get what you want. Everyone's happy. There, I'll make you a present of that suggestion."

"Why?" he asked, watching her carefully. "Why make me a present of something that might give me the break-through to Peter? Don't you want him to stay here with you, after all?"

"Of course I want him to stay here, but only if he wants to. I don't want him opting for me only because he never got to know *you*. Now why don't you come home before it starts to rain and you get soaking wet—again?"

She said the last word significantly, and Gavin looked up at her. "Again?" he asked.

"Oh, of course, I was forgetting. You don't remember, do you?"

He managed a wry grin. "Perhaps I do. I suppose I ought to thank you."

"Well, don't kill yourself doing it. Just don't get wet. I won't rescue you a second time."

"Thank you for the first time, anyway. I could have got pneumonia."

"Don't pile it on," she said, laughing. "You might have caught a small chill, but no more."

"No, I'd have caught a big chill. Unfortunately it's the way I'm made. The slightest little thing and I go down with something nasty."

She cast a curious glance at his big, sturdy frame, redolent of health and vitality, looking as if it could withstand a siege. Who would ever have dreamed it housed this secret weakness? "It must be a great inconvenience to a tycoon," she said, "wheeling and dealing—and the things tycoons do—all threatened by the sniffles."

"I don't have sniffles. I take things to hide the symptons until I have time to be sick."

"And when is that?"

"Usually never. By the time I *have* time, I'm over it anyway. Perfectly simple."

"Is it? Do you really get over it? Or are all those little maladies waiting to join together and sock it to you?"

"Now you stop that," he said, amused. "I'm not one of your sick donkeys."

"Donkeys aren't the only creatures in the world that get sick," she pointed out. "There's such a thing as being sick at heart, and it's much worse than pneumonia."

"C'mon, stop psychoanalyzing me. I'm not sick at heart or sick in any other way, and I don't need looking after."

The smile died from her face. "I think you do," she said softly. "I don't think anyone's ever really looked after you in your life."

He shrugged. "Liz tried. I wouldn't let her."

"Why?" she asked curiously.

"Because..." It was on the tip of his tongue to tell her that once he gave in to being cared for it could become a drug from which he'd never want to free himself. But, as so often was the case, caution intervened, and he simply said, "Because I didn't need to be looked after."

"But she needed to do it," Norah pointed out. "Liz had a powerful need to care for others. I learned that about her very quickly." She hesitated before saying, "Maybe that's what Dad offered her that you couldn't."

"Nonsense," he said shortly.

"I don't think so. I think you don't know how to let yourself be looked after, and you're sick from the lack of it."

He looked away from her, out to sea where the setting sun was turning the water red. It was at moments like this that she was most dangerous, for the idea of being lovingly cared for was suddenly more seductive than beauty, more alluring than perfume, more vital than life. The sweet warmth flowed from her in a river that threatened to engulf him and drag him down to his doom, to the place where weakness lay in wait.

"It's time I was getting back," he said.

To his relief she didn't try to pursue the subject, and they talked about indifferent things on the way back.

That night he awoke shivering. He was submerged in a black misery from which there seemed no escape. He vaguely sensed that it was connected with a dream he'd been having, but he couldn't remember a single detail of it. He only knew that he'd been in hell and that hell's tentacles still reached out beyond sleep, threatening to pull him back. He got out of bed and went to the bathroom to splash water on his face. He remembered a file he was working on and decided to fetch it. Anything was better than going back to sleep.

Norah had worked late that evening. As soon as one job was finished, she found another one to do. She knew time was passing and the rest of the house had gone to bed, but she kept on inventing tasks, delaying the moment she knew she would soon have to face.

At last she gave up putting it off and sat down at her father's desk and took out his papers. She'd been through his diary once already, but nothing seemed to have stuck in her brain. Now she knew she must try again, not just the diary but his next book. His publisher had called her that afternoon, gently asking if the book would have to be abandoned. But Norah resisted the idea. She wanted to see Tony's last work published as his final memorial.

He'd finished the first draft of the manuscript, but it needed revising, and she could do that through the extensive notes he'd left—not only written notes, but the ones he'd dictated into a small machine that went everywhere with him. It had been recovered from the car and given back to her, but she'd placed it in the desk without looking at it. She'd promised herself that she'd listen when she could face it, and now she must summon up her courage.

She took out the machine and discovered that it was undamaged. She switched it on and there was Tony's voice, cheerful, humorous, talking about the birds he'd seen a few hours before he died. She listened, her heart aching.

The diary was even more painful. The moment she opened it he seemed to be there, in the irreverent notes he'd made against every entry.

Remember to call Harry—try not to go to sleep when he tells me the story of the baboon for the fiftieth time.

She could hear him saying it in the voice that had always seemed on the edge of a chuckle. In her young girlhood they'd been everything to each other, forging a bond that even his marriage hadn't shaken. And Liz had been wise enough to understand that. She'd never been jealous or tried to come between them, understanding that she and Norah each held a different part of Tony's heart, which was why they got on so well together.

And now they were both gone forever: Tony, with his booming laugh, his huge love of life, and Liz, with her beauty and dizzy charm. The home that had been so warm and happy had been ripped apart, and she would never see either of them again. Suddenly the pain that had possessed Norah's heart for weeks leaped up to her throat, tightening it in a grip of agonizing intensity. She gasped, feeling the sobs fighting to the surface, tearing her apart. She pressed her hands to her mouth and the hot tears flooded over them. Her chest heaved painfully. She tried to cling onto some sort of control, not to make a noise in case she awoke Peter. At this moment she was the strong, safe point in his life, and the evidence of her grief would frighten him if he saw it. But there was no way she could control what was happening to her. It was like being buffeted by a whirlwind.

She'd cried when she first heard of the accident, but it hadn't been like this. The effort to sob silently seemed to throw her body into spasms, making her clutch the desk. Only once in her life before had this happened, when she was eight and her mother had died. But then Tony had been there with his strong arms that had held her tight, shutting out fear and misery, carrying her into a world where they could love and grieve together. But Tony would never be there to comfort her again, and suddenly she was terrified that her strength wouldn't be enough for the road ahead that was full of so many problems.

Her surroundings receded. She was only dimly aware of the door being pushed open and Gavin standing there. "What is it?" he asked. Then horror seemed to overtake him, as he saw her face. "Norah," he stammered. "What on earth...?"

But it was clear that she couldn't hear him any more. Her whole body was trembling uncontrollably. There was only one thing for him to do, so he did it, crossing the room quickly and putting his arms about her. A moan broke from Norah. It went on and on, not rising or falling, but intensifying until it dissolved into violent sobs. Gavin tightened his arms and pulled her head against his shoulder.

At first her body was stiff against him, but gradually he felt her relax and yield to her grief. He stroked her hair, wondering at her, wondering at himself. She'd seemed so strong, more than strong enough to stand up against grief, comfort Peter and fight himself at the same time. He'd thought of her as stiffened by a backbone of ice, but the slim body in his arms now was warm and soft, molding itself against his like an animal seeking comfort.

"Norah," he said uncertainly, "Norah..."

But she couldn't hear him, and he gave up trying to talk and just caressed her, stroking her hair and her wet cheeks and waiting until the storm subsided. "Norah," he said again.

She lifted her face, streaming with tears. "I can't— stop..." she choked.

"Then don't try. Go on. Let it happen. You've held this in for too long."

"But I—mustn't..."

"Who says you mustn't? You need to." He drew her close again and held her, rocking gently back and forth while her anguish expended itself against his shoulder. After Peter's quiet self-containment, he could almost have thanked Norah for needing him.

At last it was finished, and she sat drained. An amazing feeling of warmth and contentment pervaded her. "Are you all right now?" Gavin asked quietly.

"I think so," she said in a shaky voice that touched his heart. She sighed. "It's very strange..."

"What's strange?"

"I was thinking of how Dad used to hold me when I was unhappy, and wishing he could be here to hold me now. Fancy it being you."

"Yes, fancy."

She drew back and rubbed a hand over her tear streaked face. "You make a better father than I thought," she said huskily.

"Father?"

"Taking Dad's place just when I needed you."

"Oh, I see." He was obscurely displeased at being equated with her father, but he supposed it was better than "grating Gavin."

"I'm sorry if I awoke you, making so much noise."

"You didn't disturb me. I was awake already. In fact I was on my way down here to collect a file when I heard you."

"You and your facts and figures," she said huskily. "No, that's not fair. I'm sorry. You were kind."

"And you didn't think I could be?" he asked with irony.

"If I did you an injustice, perhaps it's your own fault. You work hard at not letting people know you can be kind. I wish I knew why."

Once he would have said immediately that kindness was a kind of weakness, but he knew if he said that now she would pull out of his arms. And he wanted her to stay there, comfortable and at ease with him. He wanted to go on holding her sweet body against his. "You should have had that cry long ago," he said gently.

"I couldn't afford to." She hiccuped, and he had to fight an instinct to gather her tightly against him. "I had to be strong. I couldn't afford the time for weakness," she whispered.

He heard someone—it might have been himself—say, "Grieving isn't a weakness. It's a way of replenishing your strength. Don't stare at me like that. I can be human."

"Yes, you can," she said in wonder. "It's just that you save it for the oddest times—and the oddest people. What you just said is so right. I wish you could remember it where Peter is concerned."

The sound of his son's name gave him a shock. For a moment he'd forgotten all about Peter, forgotten everything except how good it felt to be close to her, feeling that she trusted him. "I'll try to remember," he said slowly. "But it's difficult with Peter. I'm floundering."

"Well, I gathered that," she said, not unkindly, but with a little smile. "I think the camcorder's a good idea and if you also—" She stiffened suddenly. "What's that?"

Gavin too had looked up at the sound of scuffling in the hall. The next moment the door was pushing open and Flick came streaking into the room. Close behind him came light footsteps, making them jump apart a split second before Peter entered in his pajamas. He seized the fox up in his arms and stood looking at them wearily. "It's two in the morning," she chided. "You should both be asleep."

Peter nodded and backed out of the door, still clutching Flick in his arms. Gavin and Norah looked at each other self-consciously, each feeling a faint regret that the moment had gone. From somewhere in the house, Osbert honked faintly.

"I suppose we ought to call it a day," she said. "When you've found your file, I'll turn out the lights."

"My what?"

"The file you came down for."

"Oh, that. Never mind. I guess I don't need it any more."

She gave him a wondering look, but turned out the lights without saying anything. Gavin seemed awkward now, and she guessed that he, like she, was conscious of what might have happened if Peter hadn't interrupted them. It was a good thing that he'd come in when he did, she told herself firmly. Life was already complicated enough, without confusing things further by yielding to a temporary attraction. In tomorrow's light she would see the illusion for what it was. Gavin would help the process by barking at her in his usual way, and she would forget the kind, understanding man she'd met briefly tonight. Doubtless he was only a rare visitor.

They climbed the stairs together and stood, in mutual embarrassment, outside her door. "Good night," he said gruffly. "I—you'll be all right now, won't you?"

"Yes, I'll be fine now. And Gavin—thank you."

"Don't mention it," he said quickly. "Well, good night."

It was only when he'd closed his door behind him that he realized she'd called him Gavin instead of Hunter. It wasn't the first time she'd used his name, yet tonight it had sounded different. He got into bed and fell asleep almost at once, and this time the bad dreams didn't trouble him.

Chapter Seven

To Norah's bemusement and exasperation, Gavin didn't behave as she'd expected the next day. Instead of snapping at her in his usual brusque manner before retreating into the office, he went out early to buy another camcorder and immediately got to work with it. She enjoyed a laugh at his early fumblings, and he responded with a rueful smile that was the most attractive expression she'd ever seen on his face.

As if he were determined to act out of character, he also adopted her suggestion for getting the best pictures of Peter. Norah came across them while Gavin was saying, "Hold Flick a little higher so that I can see her properly.... Now let her run free.... You'd better chase her."

She laughed with pleasure, and they both looked in her direction, smiling. She tried to back off, not wanting to intrude, but Peter ran to her eagerly, took her hand and drew her before the lens. She was about to protest that this was about him, when she remembered the little subterfuge Gavin was practicing at her own suggestion. So she played along, leading Gavin through the sanctuary and asking Peter to fetch out various animals for their moment of stardom.

Delighted, she saw how father and son relaxed when they forgot to worry about their relationship. Gavin seemed to be still the gentle, kindly man of the night before, and Peter responded, smiling, and once even laughing out loud.

The next moment she wondered at herself for being pleased. Every moment that Peter seemed to be at ease in his father's company was a moment nearer the time she would lose him. Soon, perhaps, the barriers would fall, and father and son would find each other again. Then she would lose both of them. But not yet, she assured herself. There was a long way to go yet.

That evening, when Peter had gone to bed, she found Gavin watching the tape on television. She stopped in the doorway to view the screen and was surprised to see only herself. She was holding Mack and smiling into the little monkey's face. The next moment Peter appeared. But to her astonishment Gavin pressed the fast-forward button on the terminals and the picture sped ahead until she appeared again, this time in close-up. Suddenly the picture juddered to a halt. Gavin had stopped it, and was holding it still while he studied her face. Norah's heart was beating madly. She took a deep breath, trying to still it, but nothing could quiet her excitement.

Gavin heard the breath and turned sharply to see her there, just as she backed away and hurried outside. Her cheeks were burning at the implications of what she'd just seen. It was a mistake, surely. Or a whim. That was it. Gavin had watched her face on a passing whim. He was probably annoyed that she'd seen him, in case she misunderstood.

She began to make her final round of the sanctuary, hoping that by the time she went in again he would have gone to bed. But as she closed the final pen behind her she became aware of Gavin standing there, almost hidden by the darkness. "I wondered what had happened to you," he said.

"I'm always out here at this time of night," she responded, glad that her voice sounded normal, although her pulses were racing.

"But you don't always stay out for two hours," he said.

"I haven't been here for two hours."

"Yes, you have. Check your watch."

She did, and was startled. Had two hours really passed while she walked under the trees thinking of him? But she'd checked the animals as well, hadn't she? Alarmed, she discovered that she simply couldn't remember.

"I—some of them were restless. I had to spend more time with them than usual," she stammered.

"Of course." He gave no sign of noticing her prevarication, any more than she mentioned how she'd seen him studying her shadow on the screen, but the truth was there between them in the darkness, making the air vibrate.

"It was a good day, wasn't it?" she said desperately.

"Fine, thanks to you and your bright idea. I've been watching the tape. In fact—in fact, I've been watching you more than Peter."

"Have you?" she asked breathlessly.

"Yes. I wanted to fathom your secret, to find out what you have that makes Peter turn to you. I thought perhaps I could learn from you."

"Oh, I see." She was glad of the darkness to hide her disappointment.

Gavin sighed. "But it doesn't work. You give him something I can't. I don't know what it is."

"Gavin, how often do you put your arms around Peter?"

He grimaced. "He wouldn't want me to."

"You don't know that. He might hug you back. He might sense that you need it as much as he does."

He came closer and gave her a wry look. "You talk as though I were one of your sick animals. Can't you meet anyone without diagnosing them?"

"I guess not. It's an instinct by now. This is a sanctuary. No wounded creature is ever turned away. And after a while you learn that most creatures *are* wounded."

She sensed him flinch at the implication, but he stood his ground. "And that's how you cure them? By putting your arms around them?"

"There's only one way to heal," she whispered, "and that is to love."

"Is that your secret, Norah?" he asked softly. "Is that why all creatures come to you for comfort?"

"Not all," she said, looking at him.

"Yes," he replied huskily. *"All."* On the last word he reached for her blindly, pulling her against him so that his mouth could cover hers.

She went easily into his arms, kissing him back and holding his body close. She knew now that she'd been longing for this to happen ever since last night. He'd taken hold of her then to comfort her, and she'd been comforted, but it hadn't been enough. She'd wanted more. Now more was being offered to her and she seized on it with shameless hunger, receiving the caress of his lips and caressing him back with her own. A deep sigh broke from her as she felt his arms tighten about her. His need was there in his lips, in the heat of his body, in the urgent movements of his hands.

"Norah..." he whispered against her mouth. *"Norah..."*

She tried to murmur a response, but he was kissing her again. For once this super-controlled man had let his control slip, letting her sense depths of passion and abandon that were usually hidden. That was the man she wanted, the one so carefully concealed behind the iron front, the true man who could set her heart alight if only he were allowed to live and breathe in the sunlight. And she was being given a chance to find him . . .

But then a chill invaded her, as she realized the moment was slipping through her fingers. Gavin wasn't just drawing apart from her. He was actively pushing her away.

"Gavin . . ." she whispered, half pleading.

"That wasn't very wise," he said in a voice that shook.

"No, I suppose not, but—"

"But we can be wise now," Gavin hurried on. "It's not too late to keep our heads and remember that we're still on different sides. That's what you were going to say, wasn't it?"

"Yes," she said bleakly. "I guess that's what I was going to say. How lucky for us both that you're a cautious man."

"I've always had to be. It's stood me in good stead in my career."

"And in your life?" she couldn't resist asking with a touch of bitterness. "Has caution enriched your life, Gavin?"

"It's saved me from some bad mistakes."

"And kissing me was a mistake?"

"Getting involved with you would be. It would be a mistake for you, too. I'm not—not a very nice person."

"You are sometimes."

"Not often enough. Go on thinking badly of me, Norah. You're safer that way. That's a friendly tip from someone who likes you."

"Oh, *you!*" she yelled. "Get out of here and stop confusing me."

He went at once. She watched him disappear in the direction of the house, fighting a desire to throw something at him, preferably something that would hit him on the head and knock some sense into him.

The wire beside her shook, and she saw Mack clinging to the other side. She sighed and tickled his tummy. "Why can't I be like you?" she whispered. "All you think about is the next meal and the next sleep, and I'll tell you something. You've got life worked out."

He nibbled her finger, and his bright eyes gleamed at her.

When she'd calmed down, she followed Gavin into the house and prepared to go to bed. But when she reached the top of the stairs she found him standing outside Peter's room, listening intently. From behind the door Norah could hear Peter's voice, murmuring soft words. "He's got Flick in there," she said.

"And he's talking to him," Gavin said with a touch of bitterness. "He can talk when he wants to."

"He'll talk to you when he's ready. Give him time."

He gave a mirthless laugh. "I thought I'd have made the breakthrough before now—long before now. That'll show you how little I know. Perhaps I should just give up and go away. Nobody needs me here."

"That's not true," she said urgently. "Don't give up, Gavin. Peter needs you more than he knows. Be patient."

He sighed. "I'll try. But it gets harder every day. Good night, Norah. I'm sorry about tonight. Sorry for everything. Just try to forget anything happened."

"Happened?" she queried ironically. "Did anything happen? I didn't notice."

He gave a wry grin. "I asked for that, didn't I? But you're quite right."

"Battle lines drawn up again?"

"Right."

But despite her words, as she went to bed Norah found herself thinking of Liz, and wondering about her first marriage. She'd been fond of her stepmother, and apart from her one meeting with Gavin six years ago had mostly taken her view of him from Liz. Now a new thought startled her. Perhaps Liz had never really understood Gavin. Perhaps if she'd understood him properly, she might have loved him better. He was a man who would need a great deal of understanding, but Norah was used to dealing with creatures who lashed out because of some inner pain. It seemed to her that this would make her the ideal person to love him. "But I don't," she told herself quickly. "Of course I don't. What's one little kiss, after all?"

Yet the feeling of his lips on hers stayed with her long into the night, and when she fell asleep the memory haunted her dreams.

When the telephone rang next day, Norah had a rebellious moment of refusing to answer and take yet another message for Gavin. But then she thought it might be for the sanctuary, so she snatched up the receiver.

"Gavin Hunter, please," snapped a male voice.

"I'm afraid he's not here at the moment."

The man made an exasperated sound. "Is that his secretary?"

"Oh, yes," she said ironically, "of course I'm his secretary. I can't remember when I was anything else."

"Fine. Tell him please that Harry Elsemore called. I'm making progress on raising the finance on the property, but it's hard when he only owns half of it. Hallo? Are you there?"

"Yes," she said slowly. "I'm here. What did you say?"

"About this place—Strand House—that he's trying to raise money on. It's not easy when he's only the half owner. It would be better if he could get the other party out. I've got some ideas about that. Tell him to call me back as soon as he comes in. He's got my number." The man hung up.

Iris, contentedly feeding rabbits a few minutes later, was startled to see Norah stride out of the house, sprint across several hundred yards in double-quick time, and storm into the wooden hut she used as an on-site base. The door was slammed with a force that nearly demolished the hut, but this was followed by a silence that was even more alarming. After a moment Iris approached and apprehensively opened the door a crack. When nothing happened, she ventured to open it further and discovered Norah sitting on the table, her arms wrapped around her body. She was totally silent, but the silence had a volcanic quality.

"What—what are you doing?" Iris ventured to ask.

Norah spoke between gritted teeth. *"I...am... calming...down."*

"Oh, I see. Well, I'll leave you to it." Iris crept away.

An hour later Gavin's car appeared. The sight brought Norah out of the hut, face pale and eyes flashing. "Find Peter something to do at the other end of the grounds," she told Iris. "Make sure he doesn't come near the house."

Gavin went straight to his room. He was tired, hot, sticky and dispirited. Nothing was going as he'd planned, and the unfamiliar sensation of not being in control was playing havoc with his nerves. He stripped off and went into his bathroom, hoping that a shower would make him feel better. But no sooner had he stepped under the cool water than he heard the sound of his bedroom door being opened and then shut forcefully.

"Hunter." He'd never heard Norah use that tone or that volume before, and it struck his ear disagreeably.

"I'm in here," he called. "I'll be out in a moment."

Through the glass panel he could see her enter the bathroom. "I want you out now," she snapped. "I have things to say."

"Then you'll have to wait until I'm ready," he called back, affronted. "Please leave."

"Not on your life. We have to talk. Hunter, I'm warning you, if you don't get out, I'll come in."

Seeing her reach for the handle on the other side of the panel he grabbed his own handle and hung on. "What's the matter with you, woman? Have you gone mad?" he yelled over the sound of the water.

"Oh, I'm mad, all right. You've no idea just how mad. But you're going to find out. Now turn off that water and get out here."

"Don't give me orders," he shouted.

"Hah! If I gave you what I'd like to give you, you'd be in the hospital for the rest of your days. *Get out of the shower and face me like a man.*"

Curiosity, as much as anything, made him yield. "Get out of my bathroom, and I'll get out of the shower," he yelled.

"And have you lock the door against me? Oh, no!"

"If you imagine I'm getting out like this, with you standing there, you delude yourself."

"And if you imagine that the sight of your body would make me want to do anything except commit violence on it, *you* delude yourself. Here's your robe. I'll look the other way while you put it on."

She averted her head and held the robe out behind her. Now seriously alarmed, Gavin opened the shower door very gingerly and took it from her. He put it on hurriedly, keeping his eyes on her back, which seemed to radiate fury. "I'm ready," he said shortly.

She stood aside, refusing to leave first, so that he had to pass before her to get into the bedroom. "Aren't you going rather over the top?" he demanded.

"I'm not taking any chances of you retreating into the bathroom and shutting me out."

"No way. I want to know what this is all about. What gives you the right to march into my bedroom and start acting like a storm trooper? Time for explanations."

"Right! But it's going to be you doing the explaining. I had a phone call this morning. Or rather, *you* had a phone call, which I had to take. I really couldn't blame the man for assuming I was your secretary. What else do I have to do?"

"Did you get me out of the shower to make an issue of this?" he demanded in outrage.

"I got you out of the shower to discuss Harry Elsemore and his plans for driving me out of this place," Norah said emphatically.

At that moment Gavin became uncomfortably aware that the robe didn't cover him very well. He instinctively clutched the edges together while he expelled his breath very slowly. It gave him time to think.

"He was very eloquent on the need to get rid of me to make it easier for you to raise money on this house. How *dare* you try to mortgage Strand House behind my back!"

"I'm trying to raise money on my half of it, which I have every right to do."

"Not behind my back."

"Why should I discuss my business affairs with you?"

"Because they affect my home—and it's going to continue to be my home no matter what nasty little plans you and Elsemore cook up."

Gavin cursed. This had all seemed so simple when he'd first planned it, and it *was* simple. It was just that Norah had the gift of making it sound underhanded, and he was furious with her for it. "Elsemore went too far," he snapped. "I never asked him for suggestions to get you out, and I won't listen to them."

"Oh, come," she scoffed, "surely if he comes up with a real beauty—"

"I tell you I won't listen. I don't do business Elsemore's way—"

"Why on earth not?"

"Because he's a crook," Gavin snapped, realizing too late that he'd said something fatal.

He was right. Norah fell on this tidbit like a lioness devouring prey. "Oh-ho, so he's a crook! But you do have dealings with him?"

"Long-distance dealings and only when necessary."

"I wonder what sort of necessity puts you in cahoots with a crook."

"I don't like the expression 'in cahoots with.'"

"Tough!"

"As for necessity... Look around you. How long can we go on like this? But the only way I plan to get you out is to buy you out."

"Not in a million years! This place is perfect for the sanctuary, and I'm staying. I've told you that before, but you suffer from convenient deafness."

"There are other places. You'll have plenty of money with what I propose to pay you—"

"There is nowhere else like this, and I'm staying."

"Look, Norah, don't force me to play dirty."

"I don't believe what I'm hearing. You? Play dirty? Surely not."

He flushed at her sarcasm. "You're damned lucky I'm offering you money at all. Liz had no right to simply assign her half of Strand House to your father, and if I challenged you in the courts I'd rate my chance of overturning it as pretty good. That's what I should have done at the start. But no, I made the mistake of trying to be fair. Well, this is my last offer. Sell to me for a reasonable price, and I'll be fair to you. I'll help you find somewhere else. I'll even pay for the transport of the animals. I can't do more than that.

"But if you insist on fighting me to the end, you'll find out what real dirty play is. I'll take you to court and have that gift declared null and void. Then I'll turn you out without a penny. Now what's the matter?"

He asked the last question in some alarm, because Norah's expression had changed with disconcerting suddenness. The anger had vanished to be replaced by hilarity. "What's so damned funny?" he demanded.

"You are. You and your illusions. Gift, my foot! There was no gift. My father bought Liz's share of the house fair and square."

He was taken aback by this, but only briefly. "Sure he did," he said, recovering. "And I can imagine the kind of nominal price he paid. Probably one pound."

She'd stopped laughing and was looking at him curiously. "No, it was rather more than a pound."

"Ten pounds. Or did he rise to the stratospheric heights of a hundred?"

"It was more than a hundred."

"So how much? C'mon, blow my mind."

"As a matter of fact I don't know the exact amount—"

"Ah-hah!"

"But I do know it was a generous sum, because I heard Liz say it was too much."

"Well, she would say that, wouldn't she, to save his pride? None of this scares me. I still think this was a gift disguised as a sale, and that means I can still get it set aside."

"Then I suggest you try." She moved toward his bedside telephone.

"What are you doing now?" he demanded sharply.

"Calling our lawyer to say you want to see him. Hallo, Angus? Can you come over tonight and bring all the papers connected with..."

Gavin waited, fuming, until she'd finished. "Thank you," he snapped. "I could have called him myself."

"Yes, but some of the things you need to know are really my private business. Without my consent he wouldn't have opened up. But it'll be all right now."

She went to the door. As she opened it, she turned and looked at him. She went out without speaking, but Gavin stared at the door a long time after she'd gone. The look on her face as she'd regarded him had been deeply unsettling. It had been a look of pity.

He discovered why, when Angus Philbeam arrived later that evening. He was a small, elderly man with bright eyes and an alert manner. Norah tactfully left them alone together, merely remarking, "Tell him anything he wants to know, Angus."

"I gather you're interested in the details of the sale of a half share in this property that was made by Mrs. Elizabeth Ackroyd to her husband, Anthony Ackroyd," Angus remarked, removing papers from his briefcase.

"I have my doubts about whether it was a proper sale at all," Gavin informed him.

"Oh, dear me, yes, it was a proper sale. The valuation was made by a most reputable surveyor. I have here a copy of his report." Gavin skimmed quickly through the papers and gave a grunt when he came to the figure. "That, of course, was the valuation four years ago," Angus Philbeam remarked. "It's probably worth rather less now. Property has fallen in price, as I'm sure you know, Mr. Hunter."

Gavin had reason to know it. It was the fall in property prices that had knocked the bottom out of his business. But as always, when discussing money, he kept his face impassive, merely remarking carelessly, "You're surely not telling me that Tony Ackroyd paid half of this figure?"

"As a matter of fact he paid rather more."

"More?" Gavin couldn't believe his ears.

"Mr. Ackroyd felt that had Strand House been unoccupied the value would have been higher, so he insisted on paying his wife an extra thirty thousand pounds on top of the fifty percent."

Gavin felt as though the roof had caved in on him. This was far worse than anything he could have imagined.

"This surprises you?" Angus asked, looking at him intently.

"Well, yes. Somehow you don't think of a naturalist as being a—a solid man. I wonder how he persuaded anyone to give him a mortgage."

"Oh, there was no mortgage. He paid cash. He was an extremely wealthy man. As a naturalist his reputation was second to none, and his books earned him a fortune. As for his being a 'a solid man'—in these 'green' days I sometimes feel that naturalists are the only solid men. They seem to rake in cash while people in the more traditional money-making occupations are losing it. It's a topsy-turvy world."

"Yes," Gavin said with an effort. "It is, isn't it?"

Chapter Eight

When Angus had departed, Gavin went into Tony's study, seeing it with new eyes. For the first time he noticed the multitude of books that lined the walls, all with Anthony Ackroyd stamped on the spine. They'd always been there, but he'd been too annoyed to notice them before.

He returned to the living room and sat down heavily. He felt stunned. All his life he'd measured success in money, and by that standard it seemed Tony was a more successful man than he was. The lawyer's last words lingered in his mind. "Naturalists seem to rake in cash while people in the more traditional money-making occupations are losing it." Everything he'd worked for was slipping through his fingers, while a man he'd refused to take seriously had become "a solid man."

And *she* had seen this coming, and laughed as she thought of his discomfiture. He groaned, resting his arms on his knees and burying his head in his hands. Suddenly the weight of his problems was too much.

Norah came into the room a few moments later, ready to enjoy her triumph. She was bitterly angry with Gavin, as much because of her own disillusionment as in response to what he'd done. She'd awakened that morning feeling self-conscious, and the sensation had been with her all day. At the strangest moments, when she was feeding or tending animals, she would have the unnerving sensation that the present had vanished and she was once more being held firmly in Gavin Hunter's arms, his lips hard and demanding on hers.

It was true that he'd backed off at once, but it had been too late to take back the feelings she'd sensed in his embrace. They were there, and if they were there they could be aroused. And she didn't hide from herself the fact that she wanted to arouse them. The discovery that he was secretly trying to raise money on Strand House had been a brutal revelation and she'd lashed out in pain.

Now she'd come to confront him, to enjoy seeing him worsted. But something was wrong. She stopped in the doorway, disconcerted by what she saw. Gavin became aware of her and looked up. She saw the confusion of emotions that chased each other across his face: first the instinctive desire to put up a brave front; followed by a weary resignation. She realized how exhausted and strained his face was, as if he never slept properly.

"All right," he said. "You made your point. I had no idea that—I just had no idea. You should have told me earlier that I was fooling myself."

"There've been so many other things to think of. Besides, it never occurred to me that you'd misunderstood. I still don't know why you took it for granted that Dad hadn't paid properly." She came and sat beside him on the sofa.

"I didn't think naturalists had that kind of money. It seems I've been wrong about a lot of things. I'd pictured your father—I don't know..." he shrugged, unable to find the words.

"I do. You thought he was a sponger," she said, but without rancor.

"It's more than that. I thought he was a lightweight. It seems I was wrong."

"Because he made a lot of money?" she asked, wrinkling her brow.

"It's one yardstick. Maybe not the only one, but it does matter. It means he wasn't sponging on Liz, the way I thought. A man who could pay that kind of price without needing a mortgage—I have to respect that, especially since I..." he checked himself.

"Especially since what?" Norah prompted curiously.

"Nothing. I'm just disoriented. I don't know what I'm saying."

"Is business not so good?" she asked gently.

Gavin sighed. "Business is awful," he admitted. "You may as well know the truth. I'm at my wits' end. Nothing else would have made me try to raise money on Strand House. I've explored every other avenue and they're all cut off."

"I thought Hunter & Son was a big empire."

"Oh yes, it's big, all right. It's just that the foundations are rotten. I've fought as hard as I know how to keep up a good appearance, and suddenly I don't care any more. It's finished."

"What's finished?" she asked.

"*I'm* finished. There's nothing else left to try. I shall have to start selling soon."

Norah was silent. She knew little about big business and had only the vaguest idea of the reality Gavin was trying to describe, but she understood that he'd learned to respect her beloved father. In her opinion he respected him for the wrong reasons, but she appreciated the way he'd been willing to shift his point of view and this softened her toward him.

She went to the cupboard and returned with a glass bearing a measure of brandy. "Here," she said.

"Trying to get me drunk again, huh?"

"Well, it improves your disposition, I seem to remember."

"You mean it makes me talk. I say all sorts of things I shouldn't."

"Does it? Or do you say the things you should?"

"What does that mean?"

"It means you need to confide in someone about the burdens you're carrying, and you won't do it unless a drink loosens you up first."

Gavin managed a wry grin. "I thought your recipe for trouble was to put my arms around an animal?"

"Buster's not up on financial matters," she responded gravely. "Besides, that only works if your heart's in it."

"And according to you I have no heart."

"Did I say that? I don't remember."

"Oh, no, you said I was a man whom nobody loved. It was Liz who said I had no heart. Strange how I confuse you with her. You remind me of her in some ways."

"Well, I came under her influence a lot. Not as much as she'd have liked, though," Norah added with a rueful smile.

"How do you mean?"

"Well, she was so elegant and beautiful. Even when she was cleaning out a pen or grooming an animal, she contrived to be elegant and poised. She tried to teach me the secret, but I was a disappointment to her."

"What's wrong with you as you are?"

"A lot, according to Liz. She said I didn't make the best of myself."

"She didn't know what she was talking about," Gavin growled.

"Well, perhaps she didn't know what she was talking about with you, either," Norah suggested. "I think you have a heart, but it's barricaded like a hedgehog, and if anyone dares approach the prickles come out in force."

He felt a strange sensation, almost as if he were blushing. It embarrassed him to be understood. He muttered "amateur psychologist," and she laughed, not in the least disconcerted.

"Look, Gavin," she said after a moment, "you're not going to like this suggestion, but think it over before you reject it. Why don't you let me buy out your share of Strand House."

"No, thank you," he said before she'd finished speaking.

"But it would suit both of us. It would make the sanctuary safe, and you'd have some money to—to use for whatever you need money for, prop up your business or whatever."

"It's good of you, Norah, and believe me I'm grateful. But I could never sell Strand House. I had to steel myself to try to raise a mortgage on it, but sell it—never." He added involuntarily, "The old man would kill me."

"Who's the old man?"

"My father. He started Hunter & Son, and he was determined to add Strand House to it for as long as I can remember. He worked here as a boy for the family that owned it then, and he never gave up the dream of buying it. He didn't manage it, but I did."

She looked at him curiously. "But that was *his* dream. What was yours?"

As he wasn't an analytical man, Gavin had to think about this. "To be a son he could be proud of, I suppose," he said at last.

Norah pounced on this tidbit of information. Gavin usually revealed so little about himself. "And his pride was important to you," she prompted. "Was he really that wonderful?"

"He was one of the most outstanding business brains of his generation and he raised me to think I could beat his achievements—"

"But that's not what I meant," Norah interrupted with a puzzled frown. "Was he a wonderful father?"

"Actually it's 'is,' not 'was.' My father is very much alive, although he talks as though he were at death's door. He'll probably outlive me."

Norah noticed that he'd avoided her question, but she refrained from mentioning it. She was discovering that what Gavin suppressed was as significant as what he revealed. "And he wanted you to get Strand House, for him?" she mused. "And when you did, that must have been a thrilling moment for you both. He must have showered you with praise."

"That's not his way," Gavin said, staring into his glass. "Putting half of it into Liz's name was a pretty dumb move, according to him, and when she claimed her half—" he shrugged, wondering what possessed him to be lowering his guard like this, but unable to stop himself.

"He blamed you," Norah said. "And he's still blaming you, isn't he?" Gavin shrugged. "What about your mother? You said she died when you were young, but you must remember something about her."

"Hardly anything. She left him before she died."

"And took you with her? So he claimed you back after her death?" Norah asked, almost holding her breath at the idea of such an uncanny parallel.

But Gavin said, "Oh, no. I stayed with him."

"She left you behind?" Norah asked, scandalized.

"I suppose so. I was only five at the time. I didn't know much of what was going on between the adults. Anyway, she went, and I stayed with my father. It was what I wanted."

"I can't imagine a child of five choosing to be parted from his mother," Norah said emphatically.

"I told you my father is a remarkable man. I must have known that even then."

"I suppose so," she agreed, sounding unconvinced. "Did you have much contact with your mother after that?"

"I never saw her again. I didn't even know she was dead until six months after it had happened."

"*What?*"

"I'd just started a new school, and my father didn't want to unsettle me."

"He sounds like a monster."

"He had his own ways of doing things, but understand this: I'm proud to be his son. I'm proud of his achievements and of the chance to build on them."

"But you haven't been able to build on them," Norah pointed out, not unkindly, but simply to make him tell her more. "Hunter & Son is slipping away from you."

"I've been unfortunate," he conceded. "Property has slumped and..." he smiled wryly, "'nature' has risen. It was a possibility I never even considered."

"But these things are outside your control," Norah said. "Surely your father will understand that?"

"He lives in his own enclosed little world in his nursing home. He reads the papers, but he takes in what he wants and ignores the rest. His advice is always impractical."

Norah felt as though a wall between them had suddenly vanished, enabling her to see deep into his heart. And what she saw there hurt her almost unbearably. Why, he was no different from Peter, she realized; a mass of unhappiness and confusion and divided loyalties. In his reluctant description of his relationship with his father he'd unconsciously shown her a tragedy, but he'd also shown much more—how frighteningly close the tragedy was to being repeated. Now she could understand many things about Gavin and his behavior to his own son, things that seemed unpleasant until she traced them back to their source in Gavin's father. After that they seemed merely sad.

He glanced up and saw her looking at him closely. Perhaps he guessed that she was beginning to understand him, because he drew back abruptly and the line of his mouth tightened. "It's kind of you to want to help me," he said, "but I'll manage."

Norah realized she'd been firmly shut out again, but she didn't try to protest. It would have been useless. She knew now that there was only one way to get near Gavin, and that was slowly, inch by careful inch. "What about this Elsemore character?" she asked, matching his cool tone.

"Forget him. You'll have no trouble with him, I promise. You can trust me on this."

"I didn't doubt it. And remember, my offer's still open, if you change your mind."

"Thank you, but I won't need to. Now that I come to think of it, I'm sure I was taking too gloomy a view. Things aren't really that bad."

Gavin was doing as much work as possible from Strand House and going to London only when necessary. Eventually he slipped into a routine of driving to London every week, staying overnight and returning late the following day.

As the summer slipped away and the nights began to draw in, the weather turned nasty. One afternoon on the way home he found himself caught up in a storm. It had been threatening as he started the journey, and by halfway it was in full blast; a real theatrical showstopper of a storm, with bellowing thunder, lashing rain and fierce winds that tore the trees sideways.

He knew the sensible thing would be to stop at a hotel, but he wanted to get home and so he pressed on, driving as fast as he dared, which wasn't very fast. One fear haunted him, that the storm would frighten the animals and Norah would have everyone out caring for them. Including Peter. At the thought of his son working in this terrible weather, fear gripped him and he stepped on the gas.

Even so, it was past midnight when he arrived. As he turned the corner of the drive he saw an ambulance standing outside the front door and he felt as if his heart would stop. He yanked on the hand brake and dashed out of the car, hurling himself at the rear door of the ambulance. One of the ambulance men tried to bar his path. "Sir, if you'll just—"

"Get out of my way," Gavin raged. "That's my son in there. Do you hear me? *Let me get to my son.*"

He thrust the man from his path and frantically seized the rear door, yanking it open. Then he stopped, frozen, staring at the face that looked back at him from the stretcher.

"It seems I got me a Daddy," Grim said, grinning. "That's cool, since I never knew the real one."

"I..." Gavin swallowed. "I'm sorry, I thought—"

"Hey, no problem. Peter should count himself lucky to have a father who cares."

"What's the matter with you?" Gavin asked, recovering himself.

"Tree fell on me. Broke my leg. So what? I've got another one," Grim declared blithely, although his pain showed.

"Then I'll let you get on. Yes, I'm sorry..." This was to the ambulance man he'd manhandled, and who was now trying to close the door.

He turned to see Peter standing on the front steps in his pajamas and robe, holding a small mongoose. He was watching his father closely, but it was impossible to say how much he'd heard. "Are you all right?" he asked. Peter nodded. "Better get back to bed, then."

But the boy shook his head and went to the door to the back room. A motley collection of wet and bedraggled animals was in there. Iris appeared. She was soaking wet, and looked pale and exhausted. "Norah got as many of them into the house as she could, and she made Peter stay here to look after them," she explained. "The rest of us went out to help, and Grim had his accident."

"Where's Norah now?"

"The storm's ripping the place apart and there's still a lot to do. She made me come in. I'm not as young as I was."

"But where *is* she?" Gavin demanded.

"She went back out."

Gavin swore under his breath and hurried out into the storm. A flash of lightning ripped the sky. The brief light showed him the sanctuary, where the wire pens were being lashed this way and that. "Norah," he called. *"Norah."*

He thought he heard a faint answering cry and ran in her direction, bent almost doule against the wind. Through the driving rain he could just make out a figure kneeling on the ground by the animal pens. "What are you doing?" he roared as he reached her.

"The wire's ripped," she yelled back. "I must mend it or they'll get out, but I can't see what I'm doing. Can you hold the torch for me?"

"Wait, I've got a better idea." He tore back to the car and brought it around to where she was, training the headlights directly on her. Osbert immediately appeared out of the dark and apparently remembering that he was a guard goose attacked the car. Gavin shooed him away and Osbert nipped his leg before retreating, honking wildly.

"Thanks," Norah yelled. She didn't seem to have registered who was with her. She was working frantically with a pair of pliers, twisting wire, trying to make the pen safe.

"Give them to me," Gavin yelled, trying to make himself heard over the noise of the elements and Osbert at full blast. *"Give them to me."*

She did so, and he fought to bring the edges of wire together and fix them. The wire seemed to fight back, jabbing him with sharp spikes until he was bleeding, but at last he finished the job. He found he was breathing hard and sat back for a moment. He could see her in the headlights, her dark hair plastered to her skull by the rain, and to his startled gaze she seemed to be naked. Then he saw that she was wearing a short nightdress that was soaked and clinging to her body, hiding nothing. With a slight start he realized that she was beautiful. Then he pulled himself together and averted his gaze.

He began to say "Right, that's it," when he was startled by the noise of something crashing, followed by a hideous braying sound. "Good grief! What's that?"

"It sounds like Buster. He must have got out."

"All right. Let's go and catch him."

"I'll catch him. You use the car to give me some light."

He got behind the wheel and found that his sodden jacket was horribly uncomfortable. He tore it off and turned the vehicle around in a search for Buster. He found the donkey at last and began to chase him, with Norah darting in and out of the beams from the headlamps. In the eerie light she looked more naked than ever, as she twisted and turned, making vain attempts to bring the maddened animal under control. He wished he could avert his eyes again, and at the same moment he was glad that duty obliged him to look ahead.

After ten minutes of this they were no nearer to getting Buster back. Gavin got out of the car. "This is useless," he shouted. "If you do recapture him, you'll probably find that Mack has vanished in the meantime."

"Mack!" she cried. "That's a wonderful idea. Gavin, you're a genius!"

"Am I? Thanks!" he muttered.

Norah vanished back into the storm, leaving Gavin and Buster eyeing each other in mutual distrust. Once he tried to take the donkey by surprise, but Buster made off, leading him a merry dance until they were both breathless and Buster was as free as ever. It was a relief when Norah reappeared with Mack on her shoulder, clinging to her.

At once it was clear where Gavin's "genius" lay. Mack gave a squeak and launched himself onto Buster's back. Norah clapped her hands to lure him toward her and at once Mack, riding Buster like a jockey, guided him in the right direction, and into the pen. Norah fixed the door and leaned against it, breathing hard with relief.

Gavin realized that the wind had dropped and the rain abated to a light drizzle. "That's it," he said. "You can't do any more tonight."

"I guess not," Norah said with a sigh. "The poor creatures, they were so scared. I've taken most of them indoors."

"Yes, Iris told me. She said Peter was looking after them."

"They'll be all right with him. They trust him."

"Come on, let's go back."

She started to walk beside him, but at once he realized she was limping. "Have you hurt your foot?"

"No, but I lost my slippers in the mud, and the ground is a bit stony just here." She winced as she set one foot gingerly to the ground.

"You'll take an hour at that pace," Gavin said. "Put your arms around my neck."

Norah had obeyed before she quite knew what she was doing. The next moment he'd lifted her in his arms and was carrying her back to the house. "Gallantry? From you?" she said, clinging on tight.

"Shut up!" he growled, and was disconcerted by the tremor that went through her body as she chuckled. The tremor communicated itself to him, going through him again and again until his flesh was singing. He knew he should put her down at the first possible moment, but instead something impelled him to keep hold of her right across the hall and up the stairs. Norah was giving him a startled look, as if wondering how far he would go.

He kicked open the door of her room, carried her inside and kicked it shut again. "Take those wet things off," he ordered.

"Just a minute—"

"Take them off. If you can do it to me, I can do it to you."

"But you were asleep," she pointed out.

"Take them off before I take them off you," he said firmly.

He went past her into the bathroom and turned on the hot shower. Returning to the bedroom he found her still dithering uncertainly and a madness came over him. He seized the hem of the short nightdress and pulled it over her head. He had a momentary glimpse of a beautiful naked body, then he grabbed her wrist and pulled her into the bathroom. "Under that water," he ordered.

She obeyed and pulled the glass door closed behind her. Gavin resisted the temptation to admire her outline through the misty glass and left the bathroom to hurry out into the corridor. To his relief he saw Mrs. Stone just reaching the top of the stairs. "Thank heavens," he said. "Could you get some hot milk for Norah, please?"

"I'm afraid I've finished for the day," Mrs. Stone said severely.

"*What?* But you're the housekeeper, aren't you?"

"I am indeed, but that doesn't mean I'm available at all hours," Mrs. Stone said severely. "That, if I may say so, is too common a misconception. My hours were clearly laid down when I took the job and it was understood that under no circumstances—"

Unable to stem the flow, Gavin resorted to charging across it. "But this is a crisis," he roared.

"Late-night crises are extremely common in this place, which is why I took the precaution of making it plain at the outset that under no circumstances—"

"Forget it," Gavin snapped and raced downstairs. He found Iris waddling across the hall with a baby badger in her arms. "I need some hot milk—" he started to say.

"In the kitchen," she called out as she sailed past with the badger leaning over her shoulder.

From somewhere at Gavin's feet, Osbert honked.

"And you can keep your opinions to yourself," Gavin informed him. He strode into the kitchen and looked around him helplessly at the glittering technology. A shadow appeared in the doorway, and he turned and saw Peter. "Trying to get a mug of hot milk in this place is like trying to get blood from a stone," he growled. "In fact, it's *exactly* like trying to get blood from a stone. *Mrs*. Stone. That woman is well named. D'you know, I asked her for some hot milk for Norah and she stood there lecturing me about her hours? I could have strangled her."

Peter nodded and smiled. There was real sympathy and amusement in that smile, and it gave Gavin a pleasurable shock. He didn't realize that in his agitation he'd forgotten to be self-conscious with Peter, and had simply spoken to him as naturally as he would have done anyone else. "You too, huh?" he asked, and Peter nodded again.

The next moment Peter had gone to the fridge, taken out the milk and poured some into a pan. Gavin watched him. After his recent experience, he was inclined to view his son's ability to heat milk with a kind of awe.

While the milk was warming Peter thrust a towel at his father. Gavin seized it and rubbed his head dry, but Peter hadn't finished. He pointed at the sodden shirt and indicated for it to be taken off. Gavin meekly obeyed and dried his torso thankfully. He had the same feeling of being mother-henned that he'd had with Norah.

He watched as Peter ladled three large spoonfuls of sugar into a mugful of milk, added some cocoa and presented him with the result. "Thank you," he said. "That's just what Norah needs. You'd better make some for yourself as well."

Peter half turned to the stove, then something seemed to strike him and he looked back at his father inquiringly. Gavin looked back, puzzled, but when Peter pointed at him he at last understood. "Me? No, I haven't drunk cocoa in years—*yes, please, I will have some*. Thank you, son."

He wondered where his wits had been wandering, to have slipped up in such a way. Peter had actually made an approach to him and he'd nearly missed it, but a kindly fate had warned him in time. He accepted a mug from Peter's hand and sipped it gently. It was dark, sweet and, to his palate, disgusting, but he smiled and said enthusiastically, "That's great. You make a terrific cocoa. I'll tell Norah you made this. Better go to bed now." But Peter shook his head. "No? All right. You do what you feel you have to. I guess you know best." He backed hastily out of the kitchen, terrified of doing or saying the wrong things and so ruining the little progress they'd made.

He reached Norah's room to find her sitting on the bed wrapped in warm nightgown and robe. "Drink this," he said, pressing a cup into her hand.

She sipped it and made a face. "Peter's a dear, but he will swamp everything with sugar."

"I know," he said with feeling. "I've got some, too. What's more, I'm going to drink it."

"You could always throw it down the basin," she suggested, testing him. "I wouldn't tell."

"But *I'd* know," Gavin pointed out. "Besides, Peter went to a lot of trouble to make it for me." He took a deep breath and said bravely, "I'm going to drink it."

"Good for you." She took another sip. "Bless him. He's going to turn into one of those men who actually know how to look after people."

"I suppose he learned that from Tony," Gavin couldn't resist saying.

"No, I think he probably inherited it from you," she said with meaning.

As always, when she was nice to him he felt as awkward as a schoolboy. He took refuge in a large mouthful of cocoa. When he came up for air he found her still looking at him, with eyes that were kind. "I haven't thanked you for helping me yet," she said. "Normally Grim's a tower of strength in an emergency, but after his accident—well, I needed another tower, and there you were."

"Drink your cocoa," he said gruffly. "Why should I suffer alone?"

She laughed and did as he bid. He stole a look at her. Her hair, which she'd dried vigorously, stood out in spikes, and he was reminded of the urchin he'd first met six years ago. The impression was reinforced by her nightclothes, which were plain and functional.

He wondered about her. Was there anybody for whom she bought decorative wear? In the time he'd been here he'd seen no sign of a man in her life, which appeared to be dedicated entirely to the animals. Astonished, he heard his own voice saying, "You need someone to look after you."

"Who, me?" she asked comically. "I'm as tough as old boots."

"Nonsense. You just think you are."

"You know nothing about me."

"I know you've got your limit of endurance like everyone else, and you're closer to it than you think."

"You mean you hope I am," she said cheekily.

"What?"

"You hope I'm crumbling, leaving you to take over."

He'd so far forgotten their enmity that this accusation stunned and shocked him. "Thank you," he snapped. "I was trying to be nice to you, but obviously that's a trick and I've really poisoned the cocoa."

"Nah, Peter wouldn't let you," she ribbed him. Then her smile faded as she realized he was really upset. "Hey, c'mon, Hunter. I was only joking."

"But I wasn't. I really felt you needed my help, but you don't trust me an inch, do you? I might as well have saved myself the trouble."

"Look, I couldn't have done without you tonight." When he didn't answer she ventured to take his hand. "I'm sorry, Gavin."

He looked down at her hand in his, and something—he didn't know what—made him raise it gently and brush his cheek against it. "You're a fool, Norah Ackroyd," he said. "But then, so am I."

"What do you mean by that?" she asked softly.

"I don't know. I just . . . don't know."

But he did know. He had a sudden memory of the kiss they'd shared, and the desire to kiss her again was almost overwhelming. But he knew if he yielded to it he wouldn't want to stop.

"Good night," he said abruptly, and walked out of the room.

Chapter Nine

Gavin awoke to find himself sitting up in bed, staring into the darkness. The dream had returned, but once again he'd forgotten it. He strained to remember, wondering what could possibly have plunged him into such depths of misery and horror, but whatever the beast was, it had scuttled back into the recesses of his mind.

Last time he had sat up for the rest of the night, for fear of a repetition. This time he refused to give in. Firmly he forced himself to lie down again and try to go to sleep. After a long time he managed it, but only just, and it was a relief when he was roused again, not by the nightmare, but by the sound of a distant bell. He sat up and reached instinctively for his alarm clock, only to discover that it was still dark, and he didn't *have* an alarm clock.

The bell was still sounding in the distance, and now he could pinpoint it as coming from the front door. He wondered who would answer it. Mrs. Stone would probably refuse as it was out of her hours, and Iris was away for a few days. Yawning, he got out of bed and pulled on a robe. Halfway down the stairs the noise stopped, but his feet kept going automatically. As he reached the bottom step Norah slipped past him, running. "It's too late. They've gone away," he said, yawning again.

She ignored him and pulled the door open, slipped outside and slipped back again with a bird cage in her hand. Inside, a gray bird with a hooked beak sat shivering miserably. "Poor little thing," Norah said. "It's been neglected. Look at the state of its feathers."

"Who brought it here?"

"I don't know. Whoever it was had vanished by the time I opened the door," she said, still studying the bird. "But there's a note."

She pulled an envelope from between the bars of the cage, and handed it to Gavin to open. He read, *This bird is injured. Please look after it.*

"Why would they do this?" he asked, frowning. "Why not wait and talk to you?"

She glanced at him. "You'd better not know."

"Why not?"

"You'd better not know that either."

"In other words you don't trust me."

"Don't be silly. I'm protecting you." She looked up as a shadow appeared on the landing. "Go back to bed, Peter. I can manage."

But the child began to hurry downstairs, and she said quickly to Gavin, "Keep him away. I don't want him involved."

She hurried off before he could answer, and Gavin turned to face Peter at the bottom of the stairs. "We'd better do as she says," he said pleasantly. "She's the boss." Inwardly he was annoyed at the way she'd classed him with Peter as needing protection. It was clear that whoever left the bird had come by it illegally, but that wouldn't bother her. Oh, no!

"Come on," he said again.

But Peter shook his head. He was watching his father intently.

"She doesn't want you involved in this, and neither do I," Gavin said firmly. "Not until I know what's going on."

To his surprise his son took his hand and came down the last step. He led his father toward the study and pushed open the door. Gavin watched as Peter climbed on a ladder to get a book from a high shelf, brought it down and began to flick through the pages. There were several pictures of birds, none exactly like the one that had been left by the door, but all similar. Peter looked at him inquiringly, and Gavin realized that from the stairs he hadn't seen the bird properly. "Keep going," he said, watching the pages as they turned. "That's the one."

They both looked at the picture whose caption proclaimed that it was a peregrine falcon.

"One of the best-known predatory birds," Gavin read. *"Kills its prey in a spectacular dive.... Under threat from pesticides...numbers still low..."*

"So where does it come from?" he asked.

Peter looked at his father, gave a small shrug and placed a finger over his lips.

"Does that mean what I think it means?" Gavin persisted.

Peter considered this, then nodded.

"Has it ever happened before?"

Another nod.

"So what do we do now?"

Peter replaced the book and took Gavin's hand again, leading him back into the hall and toward the stairs. "You mean we just go back to bed, like good boys, because she told us to?'' Gavin demanded.

Something that might have been a smile touched Peter's face briefly. Gavin sighed. "Then I guess that's what we'd better do," he said.

To his delight Peter smiled at him again, and there was something conspiratorial about his manner that warmed his father's heart. "Women, eh?" he ventured.

Peter gave a sigh that exactly matched Gavin's, and for a moment the time and circumstances vanished and they were simply two males, wary of the female, joined in the ancient male camaraderie that had existed since time began. Some instinct warned Gavin not to press any further. Already tonight he'd been granted more than he'd hoped. He put his hand lightly on his son's shoulder and they went up the stairs together.

He didn't see Norah at breakfast next morning, but he found her in the sanctuary tending the falcon. "Is he all right?" he asked.

"Far from it. He's been disgracefully neglected, probably by someone who thinks it's clever to keep an exotic bird but can't be bothered to care for it." Her voice was full of anger, but it was a different kind of anger than the one she used on him. In their rows she'd often addressed him with exasperation, indignation and disbelief that anyone like himself could exist. But he'd never before heard the bitter hatred that she reserved for someone who ill-treated a bird or animal. "He's got a broken wing," she said, "and it's been broken for some days. All right, boy. Gently, now," she broke off to murmur at the bird. "Poor Perry. Soon have it better."

"Perry because he's a peregrine falcon, no doubt?" Gavin hazarded.

She looked up at him. "Fancy you knowing that. All right, Perry. Keep still. Not much longer."

"How do you know he escaped, at all?" Gavin asked. He couldn't bring himself to call it Perry. "It might have been living wild."

"Not in this area. He's been through human hands, and if I knew whose I'd go visiting with a gun."

"Aren't you going to call a vet?"

"No need. I can heal a broken wing, and there's nothing else wrong."

"And besides, a vet might know of a missing bird?" he asked shrewdly.

She scowled at him, but said nothing.

"You know you could be in serious trouble, don't you?" he said, exasperated.

"Why is that?"

"Because this bird was obviously stolen."

"There's no obviously about it," Norah said with a touch of defiance. "He escaped and was left on the doorstep by someone who was in too much of a hurry to wait around. I haven't heard of a stolen bird."

"And if you had, you wouldn't let on?"

She faced him angrily. "Nobody has the right to keep a creature like this in captivity, much less neglect it. And something that shouldn't be 'property' can't be stolen."

He briefly considered arguing with this flawed logic, but abandoned the idea at once. Norah had her own way of looking at the world, and a man could go crazy arguing with her. Gavin walked away without answering. After a few steps he looked back, but she was concentrating on Perry and seemed to have forgotten him.

The events of the night before had left him feeling cheered. For once Peter had offered him a glimpse into his mind, without being prompted. Normally he was forced to observe his son closely for any sign that offered a window into his thoughts. It was no use doing this when Peter was aware of him, because the child was on guard, but sometimes he could catch him unaware with lucky results. That was how they came to see *Lady and the Tramp.*

"Shall we go to that?" he asked Peter when he found him looking at the advertisement in the local paper, a couple of days later. "It's very good." Peter regarded him strangely, evidently surprised by this knowledge. "I saw it when I was a child," Gavin added, inwardly thanking the aunt who'd insisted on dragging him to the cinema. He hadn't wanted to go, condemning cartoons as "for kids"—he'd been nine at the time. But once there he'd secretly enjoyed the film, never suspecting that it would benefit him in the future.

So they went into town hoping to catch the early evening show, but the cinema was full. Unwilling to disappoint Peter Gavin took him for a snack, then they went to the late show. From time to time he glanced at him during the film. Peter never laughed, but sometimes he smiled, and Gavin was satisfied. He was learning to go slowly.

They got back to find a strange vehicle parked outside the house. It was a blind-sided van that looked as if it had seen better days. Gavin frowned and took Peter inside.

The house was quiet, but as soon as he entered he knew there was something wrong. The silence was the wrong *kind* of silence and the next moment it was broken by a gasp that sounded as if someone was in pain. Next came a man's voice with an unpleasant, smug sound. "You don't like that, do you? Well, you've only got to tell me what I want to know...."

Two quick steps took Gavin to the living room. At first he couldn't see Norah, just a very large man who seemed to be leaning against the wall. Then he realized that the man was holding Norah's wrists and crushing her slender body with his huge one. "Come on, tell me," he demanded, pressing harder and forcing a gasp of pain from her.

A red mist seemed to come before Gavin's eyes. For a moment he felt capable of killing, but he controlled himself and tapped the man on the shoulder. "Excuse me," he said politely, and when the man turned Gavin jerked his knee up swiftly. It was over in seconds. The man fell, clutching himself and cursing.

"Look after her," Gavin ordered Peter, who sprang to support Norah. He took the man by the ear. "It's the police for you," he said.

Through his pain the intruder managed to give a vicious grin. "I don't think so. Ask *her* if she wants the police." Gasping and holding onto Peter, Norah managed to shake her head. "Nah, they might ask too many questions about stolen property. Why don't you...?"

His words ended in a howl, as Gavin gripped his ear and dragged him outside. What followed was short but extremely satisfying and finished with the stranger driving off, holding the steering wheel with one hand and trying to staunch the blood from his nose with the other. Gavin tidied himself up as much as possible and went back inside. Norah was lying on the sofa, clutching her ribs. Her face was very pale. "Are you all right?" Gavin demanded abruptly.

"Yes, thank you," she said weakly. "Thank heavens you came."

"Do you know who he is?"

"He said his name was Jake Morgan. He says his falcon was stolen, and he'd heard that it might be here. I told him to go to..." Norah hesitated, her eyes on Peter "...to go away."

"I can imagine. Now I'm going to call the doctor."

"Nonsense," she said brightly. "I'm fine. I was only a little breathless, and it's over. Peter, it's time you went to bed."

The boy seemed unwilling, and it was obvious he was concerned for her. But Gavin could see she was putting on an act for his benefit, and it was fast becoming a strain. "Go on," he said to his son. "I'll look after Norah." Peter looked up at him. "She'll be safe in my hands, I promise."

Reluctantly Peter departed. As soon as the door had closed behind him, Norah fell back against the cushions. Her face was gray. "You madwoman," Gavin said harshly. "Why do you take such risks?" The sight of her pain hurt him. Even worse was the thought of what might have happened if he hadn't arrived home. "I'm calling a doctor whether you like it or not," he said, picking up the phone.

"All right. Thank you."

He summoned the doctor, who said he was on his way. When he'd put the phone down he said, "And now I ought to call the police."

"No, Gavin, *please*. It's over."

"I doubt it. He's a nasty piece of work. He won't let it be over. I'm surprised he didn't search the place."

"He did," Norah told him. "I told him he was free to."

"And he didn't find Perry?"

"I moved Perry this morning."

"Where?"

"Friends of mine who often help out at times like this."

"Have I stumbled on an underground railway for escaped birds—'escaped' in quotes?"

"Something like that. This isn't the only sanctuary in these parts, and we all help each other out."

"Evidently he suspected the truth?"

"I'm afraid so. That's what he was trying to get me to tell him."

"Did you actually deny that you'd had Perry?" Gavin asked curiously. It was hard to imagine her telling a direct lie, but even harder to imagine this passionately protective woman endangering those she'd sworn to defend.

"I told him I wouldn't dignify his suspicions with an answer," she said.

"Neat. But I doubt it'll satisfy him. You know you're getting into deep water, don't you?"

"Listen, Hunter, I will not return Perry to that man. You saw his way with something weaker than himself."

He had, and it had scared him for her sake. But what had scared him even more was the strength of his own reaction. The sight of Norah in pain had done something devastating to him, making him feel that no punishment was bad enough for the man who could hurt her. All nonsense, of course, because she'd brought her troubles on her own head. But that was logic, and increasingly logic played no part in his dealings with this woman.

"You'd better get to bed," he said, roughly to cover his sudden confusion. "I'll bring the doctor up."

He helped her to her feet, but she refused his help as she climbed the stairs, although he could tell she was in pain. The doctor arrived half an hour later. Gavin directed him upstairs and waited below until he came down.

"One slightly cracked rib. Apart from that, just bruises," he said cheerfully. "She'll have to be more careful on these stairs."

"Stairs?" Gavin echoed.

"Falling downstairs. She could have been badly hurt."

"Yes," Gavin said grimly. "She could."

He tried to tackle Norah on the subject when she came down next morning, but without success. She simply refused to discuss it, insisting, Micawber-like, that the matter was over and there was nothing to worry about. It was hard for Gavin to make an issue of it when Peter was about, listening.

A couple of days later an urgent call forced Gavin to drive to London to sort out a complication with the bankers. He returned in the early evening. While he was still a hundred yards from the house the front door was pulled open and Peter came flying down the path toward his father's car. Gavin stopped and opened the passenger door. "What is it?" he demanded urgently, but Peter simply stared at him wild-eyed. "Peter, you must talk to me. What's happened?"

Peter gave a kind of gasp, then blurted out, *"Policeman."*

"What about a policeman?" Gavin asked urgently, thanking heaven that his son had found his tongue at last.

But his relief was premature. Peter managed to say "policeman" once more in a desperate voice, but that was all. Luckily Mrs. Stone had appeared and was waiting on the doorstep. She looked upset and disapproving. "The police were here an hour ago," she told Gavin in an agitated voice. "They've arrested Norah and taken her to the police station."

Gavin was half out of the car, but at this he got back in. "Where is it?" he demanded in a taut voice.

Mrs. Stone told him and Gavin restarted the engine. Peter had settled himself in the passenger seat, but Gavin opened the door. "I don't want you at the station," he told his son. "You stay here."

Peter looked at him, his jaw set and determined in a way that reminded Gavin uncannily of his own father. But for the moment he had no attention to spare. His mind was full of dread for Norah. "You'll help her best by letting me get on with the job," he said, and Peter left the car at once.

As he drove he raged: stupid woman! She'd brought this all on herself and it would serve her right if he left her to stew in her own juice. But even as he thought it, he stepped on the gas.

At the station he found himself talking to an exasperated police sergeant. "Yes, we have Miss Norah Ackroyd here, and the only reason we know her name is that she's well known because of the sanctuary. Not one word has she spoken since we brought her in, not even when she was charged. She wouldn't even notify her lawyer. Still, you're here now. Perhaps you can make her see reason."

"I—yes," Gavin responded, gathering his wits. He'd been wondering if he'd be allowed to see her, but since he'd evidently been taken for the lawyer, he'd use any method that worked. "What exactly is the charge?"

"Theft. A Mr. Jake Morgan has produced evidence that she's harboring a peregrine falcon that was stolen from him, and that she's concealing it from him."

Gavin snorted in what he hoped was a convincingly contemptuous manner. "Evidence!"

"We've got a man who admits leaving it on her doorstep," the sergeant said. "But it's not in the sanctuary now, and she won't say where it is."

Outwardly Gavin remained cool, but inwardly he was cursing the man who'd dumped the bird on Norah and then betrayed her. "I'd like to see Miss Ackroyd now," he said.

A few minutes later he was conducted to an interview room where he found Norah sitting at a table with her jaw set stubbornly. She looked startled when she saw him, but said nothing until the door had closed and they were alone.

"I won't waste my time giving you my opinion of your common sense," Gavin declared. "They think I'm your lawyer, or I wouldn't have been allowed in. Why didn't you send for Angus Philbeam?"

"Because he'd have been useless," Norah said flatly. "Dear old Angus is a paperwork man. He'd have flapped and fuddled and advised me to confess everything."

"Instead of which you refused to say anything about this bird—"

Norah's eyes flashed. "Bird? What bird? I don't know anything about any bird."

He ground his teeth. "They've got the person who left it on your doorstep. And don't say, 'what doorstep?'"

"I don't know anything about a missing bird," she repeated defiantly.

Gavin closed his eyes and prayed for patience. When he felt calm enough to speak he said, "You were right not to send for Angus. You're going to need someone a bit sharper to get you out of this mess."

"I'm not in a mess. They can't prove anything."

"Fine," he snapped in exasperation. "Tell that to the judge and see what you get. It would serve you right if I left you to rot."

"Do so, then," she snapped back.

"Right."

"Right."

They glared at each other.

"For pity's sake, how can I just walk out and leave you?"

"Why not? You want to."

"Yes I do, but I have to face my son. He expects me to save you from the results of your own foolishness, so that's what I'm going to do."

"How?"

"I don't know."

He'd never felt so confused in his life. He was furious with her for letting this come about, but he also knew a reluctant admiration for her courage. They could lock her up and throw away the key, but she wouldn't yield an inch in defense of what she felt was right. But the feeling that possessed him most strongly was an aching protectiveness at the sight of her pale face and the frightened eyes that belied her show of defiance. If this was how she felt about the creatures she cared for, then it was no wonder she was prepared to go to the stake for them. For a searing moment he understood everything in her mind: the fear, the determination, the desperate forgetfulness of self. He understood it because he felt it, too, but not for the animals. For her.

"How's your rib?" he asked.

"It's fine," she said.

"You look very pale."

"Prison pallor," she said, attempting a joke. But she couldn't quite manage it and her voice shook.

"I'll tell them to get you a doctor."

"Gavin, the only thing I'm really worried about is the animals. Mrs. Stone won't go near them, and without Iris or Grim there's only Peter. He can't manage everything alone."

There was a silence. Gavin knew what was coming, but part of him still couldn't believe it. An irresistible fate was marching him toward the inevitable. He didn't want to go, but there was nothing he could do about it.

Hardly able to believe that the words coming out of his mouth were his own, he said, "I'll take care of the animals tonight. Don't you worry about anything."

Chapter Ten

He reached home to find Peter busy in the kitchen, mixing and mashing food with the calm air of an expert. Gavin knew a surge of admiration for his son. "I saw her," he said when Peter looked up at him. "She's all right, bearing up very well, in fact. We don't have to worry about her." But the bright words faded on his lips with the look Peter gave him. The little boy saw through everything. In many ways he wasn't a child at all, but a small adult, mature enough to fulfill his responsibilities in the midst of trouble. Gavin had to admit to himself that the Ackroyds had taught him that, at least. Peter deserved the truth.

"She's as stubborn as a mule," he said, caught between despair and exasperation. "She won't do a thing to help herself. The only thing—the *only* thing she cares about, is who's going to take care of the animals."

Peter's puzzled look said, *But, of course.*

"Well, it may be obvious to you," Gavin told him, "but somebody has to think about all the other things." He saw

Peter point a tentative finger at him. "Yes, me. She needs a lawyer. A good one. Not Angus Philbeam. Someone really high powered." Peter's eyes, fixed on him, were unnerving in their trust and expectancy. "There's always Bruce Havering," Gavin mused. Peter put his head on one side in query. "Bruce Havering is a top lawyer," Gavin explained. "He costs the earth, but earns every penny. Luckily he owes me a favor."

Peter was silent, but his eyes said, "So call him."

"It's not that easy," Gavin said defensively. "He only takes very big cases. If I ask him to dash up here for a small case in a minor court, he'll think I'm crazy."

Well, aren't you? his heart prompted.

He knew that telling Peter about Bruce had taken him beyond the point of no return. Now he had to make the call because Peter would never forgive him if he didn't. He went through into the study, Peter trotting after him. Seated at the desk, he reached for the phone, but stopped with his hand on the receiver. An astonishing thought had just come to him.

This was it, the chance he'd been hoping for ever since the day he came here, the chance to get his son back. All he had to do was do nothing at all. She would be found guilty of theft, and armed with that ammunition he could persuade the Social Services, the courts and anyone else who might want a say that she was unfit to rear his son. He had the perfect weapon in his hand, and she'd placed it there herself.

So why hadn't he given it a thought until this minute? Why was he so instinctively sure that he couldn't possibly use it?

He found one answer in the sight of Peter's shining eyes as he watched, evidently confident that his father could come galloping to Norah's rescue. For the first time he was a hero to his son, but only because he was helping her. The irony wasn't lost on him. And he knew that if he stooped to get the boy back in this way, he would also lose him forever in the only way that mattered.

And there was another answer. It lay in the thought of Norah's pale face and frightened eyes, and the bravado with which she tried unsuccessfully to hide her fear. It lay, too, in the turmoil in his own heart when he thought of her in prison, crushed like a captive bird.

He tried to tell himself that this was nonsense. It was her first offense. They wouldn't send her to prison.

But she was behind bars *now*, quietly going crazy with dread and misery, yet still not prepared to yield an inch. He took up the phone and dialed. The phone rang for so long that he was filled with dismay, but at last there was an answer. "Bruce? Sorry to call you so late."

"You just caught me," boomed the lawyer's cheerful voice. "Did I tell you Elaine and I bought a villa in Italy? We're off for our first vacation there tomorrow. Sun, sand and *vino*."

Sweat stood out on Gavin's forehead. "Look Bruce, this is an emergency..." Hurriedly he explained the situation. "She'll be up in front of the magistrates tomorrow morning."

"Tomorrow morning I'll be on the plane to Italy," Bruce said firmly.

"I don't care what it costs—"

"It'll cost my neck, if I have to explain a delay to Elaine."

"But there needn't be a delay," Gavin said, improvising madly. "She can still fly out tomorrow and you go the next day. She surely won't mind that?"

"She'll mind coping with three young children alone on the plane. No dice."

"Bruce, I hate to remind you that you owe me a favor, but this is life-or-death."

"Well, of all the—"

"Life-or-death," Gavin repeated firmly.

There was silence. "She must really be some lady."

"That's an understatement."

"Well, I guess that changes things. If you'd explained that you were in love with her—"

"I'm not," Gavin interrupted firmly. He glanced at Peter and found the boy had been momentarily distracted by Mrs. Stone who was trying to get him to come to supper. Turning away and covering his mouth with his hand, he said rapidly, "I am most emphatically not in love with Norah Ackroyd. The mere idea would be laughable if it weren't outrageous. She's a thorn in my side, a burr in my skin, a nuisance in my hair. If she got put away for life, it would be no more than she deserved. *Now will you come here and get her off?*"

Bruce chuckled. "Sure, I will. Give me the facts again, with all the details this time."

Gavin told the story to the accompaniment of grunts from Bruce. "Okay," the lawyer said at last. "Now here's what you do. See her as fast as you can tomorrow morning and tell her to go on saying absolutely nothing. I'll do all the talking. In the meantime you've given me some ideas. See you tomorrow."

Gavin put down the phone. Peter hurried back to his side. He didn't utter a word, but his eyes spoke volumes. "He's coming," Gavin said.

The next moment he was engulfed in an ecstatic hug. Peter had hurled himself onto his father, wrapping his arms tightly around his neck and almost choking him in his joy. Gavin embraced his son fiercely, almost overwhelmed by the rush of emotion that swept him. It was the first spontaneous hug from his child that he could remember in years, and he found that his eyes were filled with tears. He tried to speak, but there was a hard lump in his throat.

He tried to control himself, not wanting the youngster to see his weakness, and succeeded well enough to speak steadily. "Are you satisfied now?" he asked.

Peter drew back and nodded. He still didn't speak, but his eyes were full of joy. "Then go and have your supper."

Peter took a few steps to the door and looked back expectantly. "I'll come in a moment," Gavin promised.

He needed to be alone to recover himself completely. Their moment of shared emotion had sent him reeling, and he had to come to terms with it. One side of him had wanted to yield to it completely, tell his son how much he loved him and how much the hug meant to him. But the other side reminded him that Peter's affection wasn't really for him. Peter was simply grateful that Gavin was doing something for Norah. That was a bitter pill for Gavin to swallow, but he must force himself to swallow it before he saw his son again. Otherwise he risked making a fool of himself.

At last he went into the kitchen, to find Mrs. Stone up in arms. Supper was ready, but there was no sign of Peter. "Gone to finish feeding those dratted animals," she snapped.

"Good heavens, yes! I'd forgotten all about them."

"Here he is. You're his father. Maybe you can make him see sense."

Peter appeared in the doorway carrying an empty bowl. He'd clearly heard Mrs. Stone's words and he looked nervously at his father.

But Gavin had learned wisdom. "First the animals eat, then we do," he said. "That's what Norah would say, and that's what's going to happen."

"May I remind you, sir, that I'm off duty in exactly ten minutes and—"

"Then leave it and we'll serve ourselves," Gavin told her impatiently. "In fact, you can go off duty now." Mrs. Stone snatched off her pinny and departed almost before he'd finished speaking. "Which leaves us on our own," he told Peter. "With all those creatures out there waiting to be fed. And do you know what Norah got me to agree to do? Yes, you do, don't you? That's why you're grinning. You're going to enjoy watching me fumble around. And don't give me that innocent look. Come on, let's get on with it."

For answer, Peter took hold of his father's jacket and rubbed the fine material between his fingers, while shaking his head. "I'm not dressed right?" Gavin hazarded. "I should put on something shabby? Okay, I'll join you."

The most casual clothes he had were still too smart for what he was going to do, but there was no help for it. When he reached the kitchen dressed in slacks and shirt Peter was just coming back with an empty bowl, evidently having made his first trip. He filled the bowl again, offered one to Gavin and led the way out.

He found that one part of him stood back and watched the incredible sight of Gavin Hunter, head of Hunter & Son, filling troughs and water bowls. The other part was totally involved, concentrating, following his son's silent instructions. He stood back while Peter made the decisions, confining himself to the drudgery.

"Is that ready to be mashed up?" he asked when Peter had filled a bowl with cereal and potatoes and sprinkled the result with some brown liquid. "Because if so, I'll do it while you get on with the next thing."

The bowl was in his hands before he'd finished talking and he set to, grinding the wooden spoon around and around. It was years since he'd taken orders from anyone, but tonight he felt only relief that his son knew what to do. Following Peter's skilled guidance was the only way he would keep his promise to Norah.

He followed the boy out into the grounds and toward the pens, where he distributed mash in precise quantities, as directed. Four times they made this trip, and as they returned the last time he caught Peter looking at him slyly, almost with mischief. "All right, I'm tired, but I'm not giving up," Gavin growled. "Not before you do. Let's get started on the next lot. Why are you shaking your head? You don't mean we're finished? I don't believe it. Yes? Good. Now, how about something to eat?"

But before they could touch the food the phone rang. Gavin snatched it up and said, "Hunter," without thinking.

There was a gasp, then an elderly woman said, "I'm so sorry. I thought that was Norah's Ark."

"It *is* Norah's Ark," Gavin said quickly.

"Is Norah there?"

"I'm afraid she's—detained. How can I help you?"

"This is Mrs. Hopkins. I found a sea gull hopping about in my garden. I think it has a broken wing."

For once in his life he was completely nonplussed. What was he supposed to do in this situation? "A sea gull," he prevaricated. "With a broken wing, you say?" He was looking at Peter, hoping for a response that would guide him, but to his dismay the child simply walked out of the room. "Are you quite sure the wing is broken?" he asked wildly.

"Well, no, I haven't been able to examine it, but it can't fly, and one wing is trailing."

"Have you thought of calling the vet?"

"I'm afraid I couldn't possibly afford a vet. I live on a very small income. Besides, Norah always collects..."

To Gavin's vast relief Peter returned at that moment and he was carrying the car keys that Gavin had tossed down on the hall table. He held them up to attract his father's attention.

"Yes, yes, of course," Gavin said quickly. "I'll come and collect. Give me your address."

He scribbled it down and had replaced the receiver before he realized the address meant nothing to him. "Do you know this place?" he demanded, showing it to Peter. "Good. Let's get going, then."

Peter stopped long enough to collect a cardboard box from a hall cupboard and a local map from a drawer, then followed his father out to the car. He indicated the place on the map, and to Gavin's relief it turned out to be barely a ten-minute drive. They arrived at last at a small cottage near the shore, to find Mrs. Hopkins standing at the gate anxiously awaiting them.

"It's at the end of the garden," she said. "Every time I try to approach it flutters away."

Peter had glided past her almost before she'd finished speaking and made his way around to the back. Gavin arrived a moment later to find his son sitting on the ground, his hand outstretched to the bedraggled bird, making soft whistling noises. To Gavin's astonishment the wild terror went out of the sea gull's eyes and it visibly grew calmer. When Peter reached forward to take the bird's body between both hands, it offered no resistance. The next moment it was safely enclosed in the box.

Peter got to his feet, nodded to his father to indicate that the job was done, smiled at Mrs. Hopkins and headed back to the car. Gavin followed, feeling like the chauffeur. His whole world seemed to have been turned upside down that day, and the strangest thing of all was having to rely on his ten-year-old son to guide him, and realizing that in Peter's hands he was perfectly safe.

On the way home he said, "You'll have to tell me the way to the vet."

"There's no need," came Peter's quiet voice. "I can do this."

Gavin jumped and clutched the wheel. His son had spoken to him for the second time that day. "You mean you can actually set a bird's wing?" he asked, less in disbelief than a desire to hear Peter's voice again.

But it didn't work. Peter had said what was necessary and was obviously prepared to say no more. When Gavin ventured to glance down at him, he found him staring straight ahead. He sighed. It was painful to be offered scraps of hope, only to see them snatched away.

Back at the sanctuary Peter got to work without fuss, putting a splint on the tiny wing, his childish hands moving with the ease and confidence of a surgeon. At last the splint was on and the bird settled on some straw in the box.

"I wasn't necessary at all," Gavin thought sadly. "He could have done it all without me, except for driving the car."

But something had changed for the better. It was there in the atmosphere as Peter went purposefully to the stove where the ruin of supper was rapidly drying out. Gavin produced the plates and Peter ladled food onto them.

"We're a team," Gavin thought. "If only it could always be like this."

He ate the dried-out food without even knowing what he was eating. His mind was preoccupied with trying to find something to say to his son, words that would express his new sense of closeness without causing the boy to hastily back away from an unwanted intimacy.

But the words wouldn't come. A lifetime of leaving feelings unexpressed had left him helpless now. The harder he fought for inspiration, the emptier his mind became.

"Peter," he said at last, speaking desperately. The boy looked up. "Don't you think—I mean, couldn't we...?" It was no use. His heart was full, but inside his head there was only a vast trace of emptiness. "Why don't you make me a cup of cocoa?"

Before going to bed that night Gavin took a flashlight and wandered around the sanctuary. Many of the animals had vanished into their hideaways, but there were still some, on trees or in water, who raised curious heads to regard him. It might be fanciful, but he had the strange sensation that they, too, were watching him expectantly, wanting him to do something for her. He remembered how sure Norah had been that they'd known about the fatal accident before anyone else. Perhaps they knew this, too; not in detail, only that she wasn't here and that she was in trouble.

Buster ambled slowly over to the fence and nuzzled Gavin with his soft nose, something he'd never done before. Almost against his will he put out a hand to stroke the rough hide of the old donkey. Two bright eyes peering at him from the branches of a tree told him that Mack was also alert and watchful. He moved on, and heard the sound of faint pattering behind him. Looking back he saw Osbert, quiet for once, standing there, looking up at him.

I could bite you, the beady eyes seemed to say. *I won't, for her sake. But if you fail her—watch out.*

Gavin gave himself a shake. It was just a goose, for heaven's sake! But as he moved on he could hear the soft pattering immediately behind him.

At last he'd been around the whole sanctuary, and he felt strangely better for it. He was ready to go in now, but something stopped him.

He'd made a promise to his son. It was ridiculous to think he need make it to anyone else. Yet some inexplicable instinct made Gavin do a very uncharacteristic thing. He stood and looked around him. Here and there he could hear the soft sound of animals moving and see the faint gleam of eyes peering at him out of the darkness. But beyond what he could hear and see he was conscious of something that wasn't many animals, but one overwhelming animal presence, and it was this he addressed. "I'm doing my best," he said aloud. "And I'll bring her back to you. Do you hear? I'm going to bring her home."

As the words died away he could hear only silence, and he felt slightly foolish, wondering what he'd expected. Turning, he went slowly back to the house, with Osbert waddling a few steps behind him. And a hundred pairs of eyes watched them go.

Gavin had always prided himself on being able to sleep through a crisis. Let others fret through the night wondering if the dawn would bring the collapse of their shares or a hostile takeover. He slept the sleep of the just.

But tonight the sleep of the just was destroyed by his worries about the unjust. It was all very well to argue that the unjust had brought her problems on herself, but somehow this thought didn't ease the torment of thinking of Norah in a police cell. Her bed was probably narrow and hard, which would be painful to her ribs. But worst of all would be the cold walls and the barred window. Sweat stood out on his brow as he thought of her suffering.

At last he got up, put on his robe and went downstairs, meaning to make himself a hot drink. But when he reached the bottom step he saw a faint light coming from under the door to the back room. Quietly he stepped across and opened it a crack.

The room was dark except for one small table lamp, by whose light he could just make out the shadowy form of Peter, sitting on the sofa. He had his arms around something that Gavin couldn't at first discern. But then the other creature moved and he saw that it was Rex, Norah's dog. He waited, listening, hoping to hear the sound of his son's voice. But Peter wasn't talking to Rex, merely burying his face in the rough coat and holding him tight, as though by this means he could get closer to the person he really wanted. And that person wasn't himself, Gavin reflected sadly.

He was barely conscious of having changed through having lived close to the sanctuary, but he knew that he wasn't going to order Peter back to bed as he would once have done. He wasn't sure what he was going to do, until Peter looked up suddenly and saw him. Even in the semidarkness Gavin was aware of the flicker of tension in his son. He moved quickly to dispel it, seating himself on the sofa on the other side of Rex.

"I couldn't sleep, either," he admitted. "How can we sleep while she's in there?"

After a moment Peter nodded. His arms were still about Rex, but his eyes were fixed on his father.

"Actually, it's not really such a bad place," Gavin went on, saying what he didn't feel, in an attempt to make Peter feel better. "It's not a real prison, just a police cell, and they're treating her decently." *How were they treating her?* he wondered. "And besides, it'll only be for one night. Bruce will be here tomorrow, and he'll get her out. He's the best there is."

Peter nodded. He might have been smiling. In that light it was hard to be sure. Gavin hesitated a long time before saying the next words, but some instinct that was new to him told him they had to be said. "I went out to see the animals before I went to bed," he told Peter. "I promised them that I'd bring her back tomorrow. They trust me. You must, too."

This time Peter didn't nod or smile, and Gavin had a sinking sense of disappointment. But then he felt it, his son's hand searching for him in the darkness. He took hold of the childish hand in his own large one and gave it a squeeze. To his joy, he felt a definite squeeze back.

"I think you should go back to bed, now," he said. But at once Peter freed his hand and used it to hold onto Rex more tightly. "Take him with you," Gavin said gently. "He probably needs your company as much as you need his."

He went with them as far as the front of the stairs, and stood watching as boy and dog went up together. At the turn Peter looked back and down at his father and Gavin smiled at him, hoping he looked confident. But inside he was praying that he could deliver his promise. Because if he failed he knew his son would never trust him again.

Chapter Eleven

Gavin was up with the dawn. Still in his pajamas, he made himself some coffee and settled in the kitchen to watch the clock. It seemed to take an incredible time for half an hour to pass, but at the end of it Peter appeared, also in his pajamas. He got some milk from the fridge, heated it slightly and offered it to the hedgehog. Only when Bert was lapping contentedly did he pour some for himself. He didn't speak, but he looked at his father, and Gavin met his gaze. For a moment the silence changed in quality and became a shared thing, full of mutual understanding. Gavin's heart beat with hope. At any moment Peter would speak and their estrangement would be over.

"Well, fancy the two of you being down so early," came Mrs. Stone's iron voice from behind them.

They both jumped. The moment was shattered. Mrs. Stone began bustling around the kitchen, jarring them both. "You should have told me you wanted to eat early, and I'd have come down."

"Out of hours?" Gavin couldn't resist asking.

Mrs. Stone snorted. "I hope I can rise to the occasion."

They endured breakfast, united by their total lack of appetite for the piles of bacon and eggs she set before them. Rex and Flick, who'd appeared from nowhere, found themselves showered with tidbits. Even Osbert joined in.

"I don't suppose she's getting much of a breakfast in prison," Mrs. Stone reflected.

"She isn't in prison," Gavin said smoothly. "It's a police cell, and she won't be there long."

"Well, who can say?" Mrs. Stone mused. Gavin tightened his mouth. Mrs. Stone was relishing the drama.

"*I'm* saying," he replied firmly. "I've got the best lawyer in London."

"He's going to have to move fast to get here before the magistrates' court opens this morning," Mrs. Stone pointed out.

The same thought was troubling Gavin. While Peter went out to start feeding the animals, Gavin called the court. Norah's case was scheduled fifth, but the ones ahead were parking offenses and unlikely to take long. Nervously, he tried Bruce's London home and found himself talking to Elaine, who informed him acidly that her husband had left an hour ago. He apologized hastily and hung up before she could tell him what she thought of him.

He went to help Peter and they worked together for an hour before getting ready for the court. Gavin started to tell him that it would be better if he didn't come, but Peter simply looked at him, silently insistent, and Gavin yielded without another word.

There was still no sign of Bruce when it was time to leave, but Gavin didn't dare wait. Leaving a message with Mrs. Stone, he drove off to the town with his heart like lead within him. He was afraid, dreadfully, sickeningly afraid, though whether he was most afraid of Norah, for Peter if she didn't come home quickly, or for himself if he failed, he couldn't have said.

They found seats, and Gavin told Peter to remain there while he went to see Norah. But this time his luck was out. The officer on duty knew who he was, knew he wasn't a lawyer and refused to let him pass. "But I've got to tell her something," Gavin protested frantically.

"Sorry, sir. I've got my duty to do," the policeman said stolidly.

The clock was ticking away. The first case was taken and dispatched in ten minutes. The next two were even faster. Gavin looked about him wildly. Without advice, Norah would do something mad—like admitting everything and pleading justification.

The fourth case came and went. The usher intoned, "Norah Ackroyd." With one movement Gavin and Peter turned to see the top of her head appearing as she climbed the stairs. Gavin tried to catch her eye, but she stared straight ahead, her face pale and set.

Suddenly there was a commotion at the back, the sound of a door banging, murmuring voices, and over them the sound of one particular booming voice that made Gavin's heart leap with relief. The next moment a very large man was sweeping toward the bench, the black silk gown of a Queen's Counsel flapping behind him.

"Mr. Chairman," he intoned, addressing the chief magistrate who sat between the other two, "Bruce Havering. I ask pardon for my late appearance—traffic jams—no disrespect to this court..." He elaborated for five minutes while the chief magistrate tried vainly to get a word in edgeways.

"Are you down to appear for one of today's defendants?" he managed to ask at last.

"For Miss Norah Ackroyd, Mr. Chairman."

The magistrate frowned. "It's rather last-minute, surely? Have you had time to study the facts?"

"Quite enough time, I thank you. I don't intend to waste the court's time. My client intends to exercise her right to a full jury trial."

The magistrate's face definitely fell. It was clear that he'd been looking forward to this case, and the thought of having to refer it on to a higher court was disappointing. Gavin barely noticed. His eyes were fixed on Norah, who'd started forward looking astounded and as if she might be about to say something. At last she looked at him and he placed a finger over his lips.

Trust me, he was pleading silently. *Forget all the antagonism there's been between us and just trust me.*

To his relief she sank bank in silence, although she still looked completely bewildered.

The magistrate was saying the correct things in a slightly irritable voice. "There's a question of bail," he observed. "I don't know—"

"I should like to draw the court's attention to the fact that my client has never been charged with any previous offense," Bruce said smoothly.

The magistrate looked at him over half-moon glasses. "There would appear to be gaps in your knowledge, Mr. Havering," he observed sourly. "However, I'm prepared to grant bail at a figure of ten thousand pounds."

There was a gasp from the court at the sum, but Gavin was immediately on his feet. "I will put up the bail," he declared, and was rewarded by a glowing look on his son's face.

He had to produce a banker's draft immediately. Bruce insisted on coming to the bank with him. "I'll drive," he insisted. "I've got some papers for you to read."

As he drove he explained to Gavin some of the real reasons he'd been delayed. Gavin wanted to cheer at what he heard, and at what he was reading. "This is wonderful, Bruce. Anything I can do for you—"

"Just let me get away quickly today. I'll give you my number in Italy, but you won't need it. There won't be any trial. I'll leave as soon as she's free. You can do all the talking and impress her."

"I keep telling you, I'm not trying to impress her," Gavin insisted.

"That's right. You keep telling me," Bruce agreed imperturbably.

It took an hour for Gavin to get hold of the draft, and it cleaned out every penny of loose cash that he had. The lack of it was going to cause him big headaches, but he was sustained by the thought of Peter's admiration—and perhaps even Norah's gratitude. Despite his protestations to Bruce, he was enjoying the warm glow of knight errantry when he arrived back at court and handed over the money.

As soon as the formalities were complete and Norah had been released, she turned to Bruce and said, "I don't know how to thank you—"

"Don't," he begged. "I haven't time. There's just time to save my marriage if I rush."

"I beg your pardon?" Norah asked blankly.

"Ask him," Bruce said, pointing at Gavin. "I should have been halfway to Italy by now, but he twisted my arm to save you. Said it was a matter of life-and-death, but he wouldn't admit why. Perhaps you can get him to say it. Or perhaps you don't need to hear it. Must dash. Bye, bye." He was in his car and speeding away before anyone could speak.

Peter flung himself joyfully into Norah's arms and she hugged him back, but her eyes met Gavin's and they held a puzzled frown.

"Let's get home now," Gavin said abruptly.

For the first time Norah wished that Peter weren't there. There was so much she wanted to say to Gavin, so many questions to ask him. But there were questions to be asked of her own heart, too, such as why Bruce's hint had caused a leap of joy and hope. For the moment she must appear normal.

As they drove home she asked, "Is everything all right? The animals—?"

Couldn't she forget the animals for five minutes, he wondered? After what he'd just done for her?

"They're fine," he said, trying to sound cheerful. "Peter and I managed everything together. I just followed him."

"Yes, he's a real expert," she agreed.

In her agitation she'd almost forgotten Jake Morgan, the man behind her troubles, but as the car turned the corner of the drive she saw him standing outside Strand House, a look of black fury on his face. "I wondered why he wasn't in court this morning—" she said.

"Say nothing," Gavin ordered her. "Leave this to me. I'm about to enjoy myself a great deal."

He was hardly out of the car when Morgan pounced on him. "What the hell do you think you're at?" he raged.

Gavin regarded him coolly. "If those papers in your hand are what I think they are, you know perfectly well what I'm at," he responded.

"This woman stole my property, and you dare to try to turn the law around and make *me* look like a criminal," Morgan shouted.

Gavin eyed him with distaste. "If the state of that bird is anything to go by, you *are* a criminal," he said coldly. "You'll never get it back, and those papers tell you why."

"What papers?" Norah asked.

Morgan made a lunge at her, but Gavin got between them. "Don't force me to repeat what I did to you before," he snapped, "even though you deserve it and it would give me a lot of pleasure."

Morgan addressed Norah. "You think you're very clever, but you won't get away with it," he shouted.

"Get away with what?" she asked, bewildered. "What is this masterstroke I've pulled without knowing it?"

"You got your lawyer to serve a restraining order on Mr. Morgan, keeping him away from both you and the bird," Gavin explained.

"Bird? What bird?" she said quickly.

"Exactly," Gavin said. "You don't know anything about any bird. But even if you did, that order prevents this nasty specimen troubling you about it."

She brightened. "Did I really do that? How clever of me!"

"You were even cleverer than that. You issued a summons against him for ill-treatment of this nonexistent bird. What's more, I dare say a little research would show that he himself acquired it illegally."

"Certain to," Norah said at once.

"So it looks as if he's going to have rather more trouble with the law than you are." Gavin gave Morgan a freezing smile. "I shall enjoy your trial, Mr. Morgan."

For the first time Morgan looked uneasy. "What are you talking about? I'm not going to have any trial."

"Actually you're going to have two—one for ill-treating the bird, and another for ill-treating Miss Ackroyd. Assault is a serious offense, and she's got the bruises to prove it."

"And the cracked rib," Norah piped up. "Don't forget that."

"You don't fool me, either of you. Why didn't you go to the police at the start? That's what they'll want to know."

He'd addressed Norah, but she—realizing that only Gavin really knew what was going on—smiled sweetly and said, "You'll have to ask Mr. Hunter. He's handling my affairs."

"Thank you," Gavin said politely. He was becoming exhilarated by the way he and Norah were passing the buck back and forth between them, their minds working in perfect harmony. She was following his lead without clearly knowing where it was headed, because she trusted him. "None of us wanted to involve the police then," he told Morgan. "After all, the bird didn't exist, *then.*"

"Now look—"

"But *you* involved them, so that restraint is off. You're facing jail."

"You don't scare me," Morgan bawled.

"Yes, I do. That's why you keep licking your lips. But Miss Ackroyd is going to do you a favor."

"Don't bank on it," Norah put in darkly.

"Ah, now that's a pity. I was hoping a little bargain might be arranged to suit both sides."

"Get lost!" Morgan snapped.

"Willingly. And as Miss Ackroyd seems to feel the same way, we'll see you in court, Mr. Morgan."

"We'll look forward to it," Norah confirmed.

Morgan looked uneasily from one to the other. "You're bluffing."

"Why should we be?" Gavin asked smoothly. "Miss Ackroyd has everything to gain from having you charged with assault and nothing to lose. In fact, as you heard, she'd rather not make a deal. She'd *prefer* to see you in the dock— wouldn't you?"

"Definitely," Norah said. "I don't suppose it's the first time you've been charged with assault."

"You've got no right to say that," Morgan howled. "And anyway, it makes no odds—they're not allowed to say—"

"It can't be mentioned in court," Norah conceded, "but the magistrate will probably recognize you, so it's goodbye to that advantage." She'd recovered her cool by now and was enjoying the sense that she and Gavin were conspirators.

"Right. We'll leave it there, then," Gavin said affably.

"Now wait, I'm not an unreasonable man. A bargain, you said?"

"*He* said, not I," Norah pointed out.

"What kind of a bargain?" Morgan persisted.

"Charges dropped on both sides," Gavin said.

"Hey, that's not fair," Norah objected. "My charges are bigger than his."

"They're not," Morgan snapped.

She squared up to him. "Yes, they are."

"No brawling, you two," Gavin said sternly, and was startled by a noise from the direction of his son. It had sounded incredibly like a giggle. He looked quickly, but Peter's face was blank and angelic. He turned back to Norah. "My advice is to make the deal and get rid of this scum."

"Hey, who are you calling scum?"

"*Shut up,*" they told him in one voice. Morgan relapsed into furious silence.

"Okay, I'll deal," Norah said. "Charges dropped on both sides."

"Then you both sign these papers and the matter is over," Gavin told them, producing a pen.

Morgan swore under his breath, but snatched the pen. Gavin watched him sign the documents that would make

Norah safe and silently blessed Bruce Havering. It was less pleasant seeing her make Morgan safe, but it had to be done. He countersigned both documents as witness. "Now get out of here," he said to Morgan. The man gave them both a look of loathing, but scuttled back into his car without a word and drove away.

Nobody moved or spoke until he'd vanished. Then, with one movement, Gavin and Norah turned toward each other and cried, *"Yes."* The next moment they were in each other's arms while Peter did a dance of delight around them.

Gavin held her as firmly as he dared, mindful of her ribs, but he longed to pull her hard against him and never let her go. She was his recovered treasure, and from now on he'd keep her safe where nobody could harm her. He wanted to say all this, but it would have to wait for later when they were alone. For now it was enough that she'd come spontaneously into his arms.

Mrs. Stone appeared on the steps and for once her bleak features were relaxed in a smile. "Welcome home, miss," she said. "I've got supper ready. It's your favorite."

"Thank you," Norah said eagerly. "I've hardly been able to eat a thing and I'm famished." She took hold of Peter's hand on one side and Gavin on the other and let them lead her into the house. Gavin exchanged a look of delight with his son, and his heart soared. They'd done it. *They'd* done it. Together. Soon everything would be all right.

It was a joyful meal. Peter didn't speak, but he smiled and nodded vigorously as his father described how they'd cared for the sanctuary together. Norah demanded to know where Bruce Havering had come from, and Gavin told the story briefly. Later, when he had her to himself, he would tell it to her again in more detail. He might even tell her how Bruce had joked that he was in love with her, and the look on her face would tell him what to say next. Or perhaps he wouldn't need to say it. She knew his financial situation and would surely guess that he'd put himself at risk to raise the bail money and free her. She'd understand the truth from that.

But he couldn't say the things he wanted to with Peter here and Mrs. Stone hovering in the background, and he began to long for time to pass.

At last Peter began to yawn, and Norah said, "It's been a long day for all of us. I'll just take a look around outside, then I'm going to bed."

Peter went out with her. Gavin resisted the temptation to go too. Let them be alone together. His time was coming. He went upstairs and at last he heard them come into the house and to Peter's room. When he went in to say good-night to his son, Norah had already left. Peter was in bed, reading. He looked up when his father came in and smiled at him.

Gavin had wondered what he might say, but suddenly no words were needed. He held out his hand to Peter. "Put it there," he said. And in perfect understanding Peter did so.

He hesitated before knocking on Norah's bedroom door, listening to her moving around inside. Finally, while he was waiting with his hand raised, the door was opened and she was standing there in her robe. "Snap," she said. "I was just coming to find you."

"Yes, we have a lot to say, don't we?" he asked, going past her into the room.

"There's certainly one very important thing that must be done before I go to bed," she told him, yawning. "Oh, I'm looking forward to a decent night's sleep. You've no idea how hard that cell bed was."

"What was it you wanted to say?" he asked, his heart beating.

"It's not only 'thank you'. For one thing, I've already said that—and for another, no words are adequate for what you've done for me."

"I didn't do anything that I didn't want to do with all my heart," he told her.

"I know. You've been wonderful."

"What was it you wanted to do?" he asked, sure she was going to kiss him, and tensing in readiness.

"Oh, that. Yes. I wanted to give you this." She reached over to her bedside table and took up a piece of paper, which she handed it to him.

Gavin looked at it, smiling. Then his smile faded. It was a check for ten thousand pounds.

"It was marvelous of you to rush out and get my bail money," Norah said, "especially since you're broke. I dread to think what you must have had to do to raise it so quickly. Gavin, whatever's the matter? Isn't it the right amount?"

"Yes, yes," he said, collecting his fragmented wits. "It's just that—it's a funny thing—until this moment I hadn't given a thought to the money."

"That's because you're generous. But I had to think of it. After all, I can afford it more easily than you can."

"Yes, you can, can't you?" he said with an effort. He felt sick, stunned. He'd galloped like a knight errant to her rescue, and her response was to offer him money. Did she think he cared about the money? Didn't she know he'd have gladly impoverished himself for her sake? To have his gesture ruined was almost more than he could bear. Everything he'd hoped to win tonight now seemed like a fool's delusion.

He pulled himself together. "Thank you," he said. "There was no need to rush to repay me tonight."

"But I wanted to. I didn't like to think of you going to bed worrying. Not when I owe you so much."

The truth, of course, he realized bitterly, was that she didn't want to be in his debt a moment longer than she had to be. Well, there was a way he could relieve her of that burden. "How conscientious of you," he said, with a blank smile. "And it's nonsense to suggest that you owe me anything. I did it all for Peter. I know that will please you."

He was too preoccupied with his own suffering to notice the light fade from her eyes. "Of course, it pleases me," she said. "It means you're gaining some understanding of him, and that's the most important thing of all."

"It is, isn't it? You'd never believe how close he and I managed to become last night."

"I'd love to hear about it, but not just now. Suddenly I've got a splitting headache."

"You must be very tired," he said quickly. "I'll go now and let you get some rest. Good night, Norah."

"Good night," she said quietly.

He left her room quickly and stood breathing a sigh of relief. For a moment he'd almost revealed his innermost feelings, but he'd avoided disaster just in time.

As for the pain in his heart—well, that was another matter.

Chapter Twelve

Gavin was on the phone when Norah's shadow darkened the doorway. He finished the conversation quickly and glanced up, no longer trying to hide from himself the pleasure he gained from the sight of her. But she didn't look pleased. She was frowning. "It wasn't very courteous of you not to tell me you'd invited your father to stay," she said.

"My father? Of course I haven't. Whatever put that idea into your head?"

"He did. He's just arrived."

"*What?*" Gavin's astonishment propelled him out of the chair and halfway across the room. "He can't have done."

"An ambulance drew up outside and he was lifted out in a wheelchair. He's got a male nurse who's also arrived to stay."

"Norah, I swear to you I knew nothing about this. You've got to believe me."

"All right," she said, her face relaxing. "I just thought for a moment that you'd summoned reinforcements."

"Reinforcements against what? I thought we had a truce—maybe even a friendship?" He said the last words with uncharacteristic hesitancy. He never knew where he was with her.

To his astonishment, she replied, "Perhaps we do. The thing is, I never know where I am with you. Now, why are you looking all struck of a heap?"

"I—nothing. I'd better go and see my father."

"Try and look pleased to see him," she said shrewdly.

"Of course I'm pleased to see him—heaven help me!"

Norah chuckled and he forced a smile onto his face before going out into the hall. "Father, what a delightful surprise!"

William glared at him balefully from his wheelchair. He was a small, wizened man with brilliant eyes. "Surprise is right," he snapped. "Knowing how I feel about this house, a good son would have invited me weeks ago."

"I always meant to, but I wasn't sure if you were strong enough. Besides, things have been in such turmoil recently—"

"Because of that woman, you mean?"

Gavin glanced at the open door and swiftly wheeled his father away into the living room. "If you mean Miss Ackroyd, she and I have learned to come to terms with each other."

"Don't give me that mealymouthed stuff," William growled. "When enemies 'come to terms' it means that one of them has given in. And since she's still here, it means *you've* given in. Why haven't you got her out of here?"

Gavin briefly considered trying to explain his new feeling that Norah had as much right to be here as he did, perhaps more, but he gave it up at once. William would think he was crazy. He settled for the only explanation his father would understand. "I can't get her out. She owns half the place."

"Poppcock! A legal fiction to deceive you."

"Her father bought Liz's share—for cash," Gavin said. He added the price and had the satisfaction of seeing William's eyes open wide in surprise. If there was one thing his father understood it was hard cash.

But the next moment William had returned to the attack. "So buy her out. Sell some of our assets. We've got plenty."

"The property market isn't what it was," Gavin said carefully. "Raising that kind of money now would be—complicated." It would be impossible, but he couldn't tell William that. "Besides, she doesn't want to sell."

"Pooh! So what? There are ways of persuading people."

"Don't let's spoil your visit with a fight, Father," Gavin said, striving to keep the smile on his face.

"Won't spoil it at all. I enjoy a fight. Where's my grandson?"

"I'll fetch him in a moment," Gavin said, "but before you see him, there's something you must understand. Peter's had a very bad time recently and he's withdrawn into himself. He doesn't speak."

"Doesn't speak? What d'you mean? You mean he *can't* speak?"

"He can, but he doesn't. He's happier in his own world. He'll come out of it when he's ready."

"Stuff and nonsense! It does no good to humor tantrums."

"I don't consider it a tantrum," Gavin said, trying to keep the anger out of his voice. "I don't push him about this, and I won't allow you to push him. If I don't have your word not to try to bully him, I'll keep him away from you."

"Bully him. *Bully him?* I'm the mildest man on earth. If I ever thought to see my own son giving in to such namby-pamby—all right, all right. I won't say a word."

"Your promise?"

"Yes, yes. Get on with it."

Peter was fetched and introduced to his grandfather. To Gavin's pleasure he showed no shrinking, stepping forward calmly to shake hands, but he remained silent when William spoke to him. In a sense the old man kept his word and let the matter go without comment, but his restraint had a quality of disgust that Gavin recognized from his own childhood. He felt a remembering shiver go through him.

Mrs. Stone announced that William's room was ready, and the nurse took him to it. They saw no more of him until the evening meal, by which time William was fully rested and raring to go. Gavin faced the evening with dread.

Throughout the meal William studiously ignored Peter. He did more than ignore him. He showed no awareness of his presence, talking rudely across him as though he were an empty space. Gavin felt his soul shrivel with sympathy for his son. He would have liked to remonstrate with the old man, but could think of nothing he could do that wouldn't make matters worse. He glanced at Peter and saw that his son was regarding William with curiosity. He didn't seem hurt, merely interested. Then he saw Gavin's encouraging look, glanced back at William, and lifted his shoulders a fraction. There was a slight smile on his face as if he were saying, "Don't worry. This doesn't trouble me."

With astonishment Gavin realized that Peter had got William's measure. He'd seen right through the old man to the petty spite that lay behind his behavior. Having assessed it, he could deal with it. For a boy of ten it was a sophisticated response, Gavin realized, and one that suggested an inner security. In fact, it was more sophisticated and secure than Gavin's own reaction to his father.

But, then, he had a history of being at a disadvantage with William. His heart sank at the thought of having his father here for a long visit, upsetting everything, just when things were going so well.

And then he wondered at himself. His firm was still in a mess. He was no nearer recovering either Peter or Strand House. So why did he feel things were going well?

He saw Norah looking across at him, a gentle, quizzical smile on her face, and he was swept by a feeling that as long as she smiled at him nothing could possibly go badly. He looked away, suddenly self-conscious.

Afterward, when Peter had gone to bed, Gavin, Norah and William shared a drink in the living room. William kept glaring at Norah, evidently considering her an interloper, until at last she took pity on Gavin and announced her intention of taking a last look at the sanctuary.

"Do you allow her to come in here?" William demanded when she had gone.

"Father, don't you understand? This is her house, too. She goes where she wants."

"Then do something about it. Did I raise a spineless milksop?"

"Probably," Gavin was goaded to retort. "I certainly haven't the nerve to tell Norah where she can and can't go in her own house."

"Then it's time you—what the devil is that noise?" A mad rapping sound was coming from the door. Gavin went across impatiently and opened it. At once Osbert waddled in, honking with irritation at being kept waiting. "Get that creature out of here," William yelled.

"It's only Osbert," Gavin said.

"It has a *name?*" William enquired with awful sarcasm.

"They all have names. It sounds a little odd at first, but you soon get used to it."

"I have no intention of getting used to it. Not here. Do you know what Strand House used to be?"

"Of course, I do. You've told me often enough."

"A place of beauty and gracious living. You've let them turn it into a zoo."

"It's not a zoo, it's a sanctuary—a place of healing and peace."

"Sentimental poppycock! Get that bird away from me."

"Don't wave your stick at him like that," Gavin said sharply. "You'll scare him."

The warning came too late. William swung his stick wildly at Osbert, missing the bird's beak by half an inch. Osbert danced with rage and gathered himself for an attack. Quickly Gavin intervened, grabbing the furious bird around the body, but Osbert twisted his neck back far enough to bite him. He yelled and strode to the door, pushing Osbert out and slamming it shut behind him.

"That creature ought to be put down," William shouted. "He's vicious."

"He's not vicious," Gavin growled, rubbing his arm. "He just doesn't like being attacked. It'll be all right as long as you don't do it again."

"*I?* Are you daring to blame me?"

Gavin sighed. "This is Osbert's home," he declared, knowing how he must sound to the man who had raised him to believe only in the tangible signs of success.

"They've addled your brains," William snapped. "You'd never have said such a daft thing at one time."

"No," Gavin said, in wonder at himself. "I wouldn't, would I?"

"So you admit it? It's a relief that you can see the truth."

"Just what truth do you have in mind, Father? I'm beginning to wonder if your truth and mine are the same. Maybe they haven't been for a long time."

William ignored this. "You admit that this place and the people in it are rotting your brains. Think what they're doing to your son. You must get him away from here while there's time to save him."

"I don't think he needs saving from anyone or anything here," Gavin said deliberately. "I'm perfectly happy with what he's learning."

"Stuff and nonsense. He's growing up. He's got to learn to be a man, and it's your duty to move him out of here and see that he does."

"It's not that simple. I explained in my letter that he's legally under the care of the Local Authority and I can't move him without their permission."

"Local Authority be damned! I've been dealing with them all my life, and I've never let them get the better of me yet."

"Yes, I'm familiar with your ways with planning departments. This is a little different."

"Determination and a refusal to be bullied will work with any department. I taught you that long ago, and until now I thought you'd learned the lesson. I was proud of you. Now I'm beginning to think there's a weakness in you. Stop pussyfooting around and take possession of your own son."

"I don't like the expression 'take possession of,' " Gavin said firmly. "My son isn't a possession. He's a person with ideas of his own."

"Nonsense," William snapped. "Children are what you make them. Look what I made of you."

Gavin swung around on him. "Yes, look what you made of me," he said bitterly. "A man whom nobody loves."

He strode from the room, feeling he couldn't bear any more. In the hall he found Norah, and from her face he knew at once that she'd overheard the whole exchange. "You were right," he said. "A man nobody loves."

"No," she whispered. "I was wrong. I was so wrong."

There was a new light on her face. Before he knew what she meant to do she had reached up and laid her lips gently against his. The next moment they heard William banging on the door with his stick, shouting, ready to continue the argument. Norah sighed and hurried away. Gavin turned to confront his father. And neither of them saw Peter peering through the banisters.

He was back in the misery and despair that had haunted his nights for weeks, plunged into a darkness in which he screamed and screamed, but there was no sound.

But suddenly the suffocating silence was broken by the most beautiful, gentle voice he'd ever heard. Hands held him and he awoke to find himself staring, wild-eyed, into Norah's face, clutching her as if she were his lifeline. And she was. He saw it now. He could see everything now.

"Gavin," she said, shaking him to make him awaken properly. "Gavin, it's all right. I'm here." Then, as he continued to stare at her with a ghastly face, she pulled him against her and enfolded him in her arms, stroking his tousled hair and laying her cheek against him. "It's all right," she whispered. "I'm here."

"Thank God you are," he said hoarsely. His face was pressed against her bare skin and he could breathe in the scent of feminine warmth and sweetness. Yet he was hardly aware of sexual provocation, only the ineffable bliss of being comforted.

"It must have been a terrible dream," she murmured, "and you seem to have it so often."

"How do you know?"

"I hear you. You cry out in your sleep almost every night. Tonight it was louder than usual. That's why I came in."

Once it would have appalled him to know she'd heard him crying out in his sleep. Now he only felt relief that she understood without explanations. "What was the dream about?" she asked.

"I don't know. I wake up in a terrible state, full of fear and dread, and not knowing why."

"If you could only remember, we might fight it together," she sighed.

He grew still, trying to absorb this novel idea. Fighting was something he'd always done alone. His idea of "together" had been with Liz or Peter, two people he'd wanted to protect. The ideas of enlisting them on his side in the fight had simply never occurred to him. Now it seemed so obvious; as obvious as the fact that there was no one he wanted fighting for him more than Norah. "Together," he murmured longingly. "If only we could."

"We can. It's not so hard."

"It is for me," he said with difficulty.

"Yes. For you. But we could still manage it, if we knew what you were afraid of."

It was on the tip of his tongue to say the old instinctive words, that he wasn't afraid of anything. But that wouldn't do, not here and now, now with this deeply honest woman. "I don't know what I'm afraid of," he said at last. "I've hidden it too deep. I'm—*afraid* to find it."

"Why?" she probed gently. "Why are you afraid to find it?"

"Because it might be more than I could bear." A shudder went through him. "Unless—unless you were there."

"I'm here," she said softly, stroking his hair. "I'll always be here."

As she spoke, he had a sudden brief vision of another nightmare—the nightmare of losing her, as though the things they would say now would lead irresistibly to their separation. "It's all right," he said. "It's over now. The dream's gone. We can't drag it back, and we don't need to."

The words were hollow and false to his own ears, and he could only guess how they seemed to her. She didn't answer, but drew back and looked him full in the face. Her eyes were kind, but full of disappointment, as though she'd found him a coward. "It's all right," he said desperately.

"If you say so."

He held her tightly, as if to stop her going, while his thoughts whirled in torment. At last he asked, "Could you ever make out what I said?"

"Not in the past. It was just indistinct shouting. But tonight you were clearly saying, 'I don't want to go. I don't want to go.' You kept shouting it over and over again. Does it mean anything?"

He told himself it didn't mean a thing, but the wall of denial was starting to crumble, and through the cracks he could see the thing he'd hidden from all these years. He could see a little boy, just six years old, dragged screaming from his mother. The child's sobs and cries tore into Gavin, and his desperate pleading to stay with the only person he loved made him cover his ears. But nothing could shut out the terrible sound because it was inside him, in the childhood self that still inhabited his man's body. It had always been there, and it always would be.

"Yes," he said at last. "It means something. When my mother left my father, she took me with her. We were happy. I loved her and she—she loved me. But my father persuaded the court that she was an unfit mother and he came after us armed with an order. He made me go with him. I didn't want to. I begged and pleaded to stay with my mother, but he dragged me away by force—"

He shuddered and her arms tightened around him in a fierce, protective embrace. "Oh, God," she whispered.

"I never saw her again," Gavin said in a bleak voice. "She died soon after."

This time Norah couldn't say anything. She could only rock gently back and forth, trying to comfort the unhappy child through the man in whom he still lived. Norah disapproved of violence, but when she considered William, who'd wreaked such devastation on the man in her arms, her thoughts were savage.

"And that was the dream?" she asked gently.

"Yes. I've blotted the truth out all my life, because it was the only way I could survive. I remember feeling so helpless. My life could be turned upside down without any reference to my feelings, and there was nothing I could do about it. I swore I'd never be helpless again as long as I lived."

"So that's why—?"

"Yes, that's why I'm the way I am—overbearing, brutal—"

"No, not brutal," she said quickly. "I thought so once, but I know better now."

"I hope you're right. Not that it helps to know that now."

"It always helps to know the truth about yourself."

"Maybe. It's too soon for me to see how that could be. All I know is that suppressing it hasn't worked. Recently, it's started to come back to the surface. I guess we both know why."

"Why do *you* think?" Norah asked cautiously. In her heart she knew the answer, but she was breathless with hope at the way Gavin was learning understanding, and she wanted to know how far he'd gone.

"Because of Peter," he answered. "My father tried for years to turn me into an extension of himself—"

"But he hasn't managed it," she couldn't resist breaking in. "You seem like him on the surface, but underneath you're more generous and unselfish than he could ever be."

"I don't know. I only know that he came frighteningly close to succeeding. I told Peter that he had to learn to fight the world like a man, and then I had the strangest sensation. It was because my father used those very words to me. I'd better face the worst now. I've turned into him—a man who's unfit to care for a child."

"Gavin, you're being too hard on yourself—"

"Perhaps it's time I was a little hard on myself. How many times have I told you that Peter had to come with me because he was *mine,* without thinking of his feelings? No wonder he turned away from me in fear. He feels about me the way I've always felt about my father, and that's the worst thing of all. That's the thing I've got to put right."

He raised his head and looked her in the eyes. His face was ravaged. "I came so close to repeating history, didn't I? I nearly damaged him as I was damaged. But I won't let it happen. *I have to stop it now.*"

"How?" she asked.

"By leaving, going a long way away, where he'll forget me."

"Gavin, that's not the way," she said quickly.

"It's the only way. I have to break the cycle and let him be free of me. I'm going to leave him with you."

"No." The cry broke from her. "You mustn't go. Not now."

He looked at her intently in the dim light. "Not now?" he asked tentatively.

She didn't answer in words, but the truth was in her eyes. He no longer had any defenses against his feelings, and for almost the first time in his life he did what his instincts were telling him to do, without question, without fear, with nothing but an overwhelming need. Drawing her to him slowly he laid his lips on hers, and immediately felt a deep peace invade him, body and soul.

She melted against him, kissing him back with ardor and some other quality, something he hardly dared to hope was love. But as they held each other and the peace possessed him completely, he knew what it was that united them. It was bitter to discover the sweet truth when he had to leave her, but he had no regrets. If he had to live a thousand lonely years without her, he would say they were all worth it for this moment, for the unspeakable joy of knowing that he'd won the love of the most perfect woman in the world.

He released her and looked into her face, loving everything he saw and trying to fix the sight in his mind against the lonely days to come. "I love you," he whispered. "I don't think I knew what love was until I met you. Norah... Norah... tell me that you love me."

"I love you now and forever," she said quietly.

"Oh, God," he groaned. "Why did this have to happen when it's too late?"

"Gavin, it doesn't have to be too late. We can make it right."

"Nothing will ever be right for Peter as long as I'm around. Don't you see? I have to leave. It's the only way to save him. As long as I'm here, he'll suffer."

"You can't know that—"

"Yes, I can, because I remember my own feelings. I've hidden them all these years, and now it's as though I'm feeling them for the first time. But perhaps I'm different from my father in this one thing—that I can see what's happening and stop it. And I *must* stop it. I mustn't let Peter suffer as I did. He's too fine and sensitive. He'd be even more damaged than I was."

"But what will you do? You mustn't go back to your old life, where only property mattered. It'll suck you in and make you hard again. Don't do that, Gavin."

"No, I'm finished with all that. Everything is hazy in my head right now, but one thing is clear. I must assign my half of this house to Peter, so that the sanctuary can be completely safe, then I'll sell out and manage with what—if anything—is left. And perhaps one day I'll be able to come back, when Peter's had time to forgive me and I've learned to be the kind of father he needs. It may not be for a long time, but I'll return one day. In the meantime, I give him to you."

She looked at him and there was a new light in her face. "You love Peter enough to give him up?" she whispered. "You really love him as much as that?"

"As much as that," he said.

"Oh, God, I've been so wrong about you."

He managed a smile. "I never thought to hear you say that. Kiss me, my love. Kiss me as if it's the only kiss we'll ever have."

She took his face between her hands and looked into it for a long moment, fixing it in her heart's memory. She knew he was a man of iron will, and she had a terrible vision of the separation to come. The dread of that empty time ahead was there in her kiss, in the gentleness with which she laid her lips on his, and the soft, caressing movements with which she tried to tell him that she loved him. She could feel his answering love in the way he put his arms about her and drew her close. The man she'd once believed him to be would have been incapable of such tenderness, but she understood him better now, knew that there had always been love and tenderness within him, waiting to be released. Somehow she found the courage to believe that one day they would find each other again. His kiss told her that it was the same with him, and for a long time they clung together in silence, seeking reassurance and strength against the lonely time that faced them.

* * *

Gavin breakfasted early and alone, drinking only coffee. When he heard the others coming he went into the study and made two telephone calls, one to William's convalescent home and the other to Angus Philbeam.

When he was sure he could control his feelings he went to William's room. The nurse had just finished getting the old man up and settled into his wheelchair. Gavin gave him a nod and the man departed. "About time you came to see me," William growled. "We have a lot to talk about."

"We have nothing left to talk about," Gavin said distantly. "I'm sorry, Father, but I can't invite you to stay."

"What do you mean, 'invite?' I'm here."

"But you'll be leaving as soon as the ambulance arrives for you. I've made all the arrangements. The home knows you're coming back."

William eyed him with disgust. "I see. Getting rid of me because you don't want me to see you caving in, eh?"

"You're leaving because I'm leaving myself. Neither of us belongs here any more."

"Now what are you talking about? I never could understand the half of what you said."

"That's because you never listened. If you'd ever been interested in what *I* thought, you'd have discovered that I wasn't just a replica of you. But of course, you didn't want to know that. You've spent thirty years trying to use me to revenge yourself on my mother, for leaving you. And I've only just seen it. But it's over. I got a lesson from my son last night. He's too secure in his own values to let you trouble him. I wish I could have said the same of myself before now, but until recently I wasn't given the benefit of knowing Norah Ackroyd."

He waited to see if William would answer, but for once the spiteful old man was lost for words. Only the mottling of his face betrayed that his son's words were having any effect.

"I'm putting my half of this house in Peter's name, and I'm leaving everything in Norah's care," Gavin went on. "When I get back to town I'm going to free myself of the weary load of trying to prop up Hunter & Son. I've done my best, but my best isn't good enough and I don't care any more. I'm going to sell what I have to and pay the debts. You needn't worry. There'll be enough left to keep you in comfort, but beyond that I have no further interest in struggling to keep up a front of success when there's no re-ality behind it."

William turned rancorous eyes on him. "Quitter!" he spat. "I might have expected this from *her* son. You're a quitter."

"Yes," Gavin agreed quietly. "I suppose I am. I've quit your world. Now I must try to find my own."

There was a knock on the door. It was Norah, to tell him Angus had arrived. Gavin went downstairs quickly, leaving Norah and William briefly alone. The old man eyed her with bitter dislike.

"You," he said. "You did this."

"No," she said simply. "You did it."

Angus had come prepared with the documents transfer-ring ownership of one half of Strand House to Peter, nam-ing Norah as his trustee until the boy was of age. Angus was troubled. "May I ask," he said delicately, "whether you are taking this course of action because you fear...er...total insolvency?"

"No, I'm not bankrupt," Gavin said with a half smile. "At least, not financially bankrupt. No, this is for...other reasons."

By the time he'd finished, the ambulance was at the door and William was already in the hallway, seated in his wheelchair and scowling. "I won't say goodbye," he snapped. "A son who could throw his father out on the mercy of the world has nothing to say to me or I to him."

"You're not being thrown out on the mercy of the world, Father," Gavin said patiently. "You're going back to live in great comfort, in a place where I've no doubt you've got everyone running around after you." The nurse's hastily smothered grin confirmed this estimate. "I'll come to see you soon," Gavin added.

"Don't bother," William snorted. "I don't need to see a failure."

"Yes, I am a failure," Gavin said quietly. "But not in the way you mean."

"There's only one way. You knew that once. But you let *them* get to you and rot your brains. You're *her* son, all right."

"I hope so," Gavin said. "I've been yours for too long. But I've remembered enough to know that my mother would have been at home here. And she'd have loved Norah."

"I won't dignify that kind of pap with an answer. You've let me down. That's all I care about."

Gavin nodded. "It really is all you care about, isn't it?" he asked. "I'm just glad I saw it before I did any more damage to my son. Goodbye, Father."

"Get me out of here," William told his nurse in disgust.

Norah came out to stand by Gavin on the front step and together they watched the ambulance depart. "I'm sorry," she said.

"Don't be. I feel as if a load had been lifted from my shoulders. Come with me." He took her hand and led her indoors to where the papers still lay on the table. "These are my copies," he said, handing them to her. "Take care of them, and take care of Peter. But I didn't need to say that. You look after him much better than I can."

"I still don't believe that," she said quickly. "Now that you've come to understand so much, you ought to stay. Peter needs you."

Gavin shook his head reluctantly. "I'd like to think so. If he'd shown any sign of opening up toward me...of even liking me...it would be different. There have been times when I felt we were beginning to get close, times when he smiled or we seemed to share a thought. But they were always isolated incidents. I never knew how to build on them. The fact is, I'm no nearer to winning his heart than I was at the start. He doesn't want me, and I can do only harm by forcing myself on him."

"But to leave now, when we—when we've only just—" she stopped, choked with misery.

"I know," he said, with a pain that matched her own. "But I have to put Peter first. Maybe when he's older you and I can find each other again. I'll live for that."

He drew her close to him and laid his lips on hers. They clung together, each wondering when they would be in the other's arms again. "I love you," he whispered, "but I have to leave now, while I'm still strong enough. Help me, my darling."

She nodded and smiled bravely. They were each thinking the same thing, that they could be as strong as they had to be, for Peter's sake.

"I've got a few things packed in an overnight bag," he said. "I'll send for the rest. Now I must go and tell him."

He found Peter playing with Buster and Mack. "I'd like a word with you," he said quietly.

Peter shut the pen door behind him and looked inquiringly at his father.

"I've come to say goodbye," Gavin said. "I'm going away. You can stay here with Norah, and I promise I'll never try to take you away from her." He looked into the boy's face for some sign of response, but Peter merely looked puzzled, as if nothing he was hearing made sense. "Do you understand? You're safe. You can stay here for as long as you want." He took a deep breath. "I haven't been a good father to you, but I've tried. I want you to know I've done my best, and when I failed—it wasn't because I didn't love you. I've always loved you, and I always will. But..." the next words were the hardest "...maybe Tony Ackroyd was a better father to you than I was." He sighed. "I guess it was just too late for us."

If there'd been a sign, a word, a look, he'd have changed his mind there and then. With an aching heart he waited for something that would give him hope, but Peter only stared at him, his face registering nothing. The hardest thing Gavin had ever done in his life was to kiss his son gently on the cheek, then turn and walk away.

Norah was waiting in the hall, her face full of hope, which faded when she saw him. He kissed her briefly before going out to the car.

She came to the front step to watch him, and after a moment Peter joined her. He stood completely still, his eyes fixed on his father. Gavin waved to them and paused a moment, fixing them in his mind, then opened the car door.

The next moment the air was split by an anguished scream. "DADDY!"

Gavin whirled around to see Peter standing there, tears streaming down his face. *"Daddy,"* he cried, "Daddy, don't go, *please.*"

He couldn't move. He could only stare in joyful disbelief at what had happened at last. Then he took a stumbling step forward. At the same time Peter began to run, leaping down the stairs to throw himself into Gavin's arms. "Don't go," he pleaded frantically. "Stay with me, Daddy."

Gavin picked him up boldly and looked into his face. "Is that what you really want?" he asked urgently.

For answer, Peter tightened both arms around his neck. Over his shoulder Gavin's eyes met Norah's. As she came close he freed an arm to enclose her, and the three of them stood there, unmoving, for a long moment.

"I guess you can't escape us," she said at last. She took one of his hands, Peter took the other, and together they drew him back inside the house.

"This time you're here to stay, my love," she said, closing the door on the world. "Welcome home!"

*   *   *   *   *

SILHOUETTE® Desire®

DIANA PALMER IS BACK!

and bringing you two more wonderful stories filled with love, laughter and unforgettable passion. And this time, she's crossing lines....

In August, Silhouette Desire brings you NIGHT OF LOVE (#799)

Man of the Month Steven Ryker promised to steer clear of his ex-fiancée, Meg Shannon, but some promises were meant to be broken!

And in November, Silhouette Romance presents KING'S RANSOM (#971)

When a king in disguise is forced to hide out in Brianna Scott's tiny apartment, "too close for comfort" gets a whole new meaning!

Don't miss these wonderful stories from bestselling author DIANA PALMER. Only from Silhouette®

DPTITLES

Take 4 bestselling love stories FREE

Plus get a FREE surprise gift!

SMYTHESHIRE, MASSACHUSETTS.

Small town. Big secrets.

Silhouette Romance invites you to visit Elizabeth August's intriguing small town, a place with an unusual legacy rooted deep in the past....

THE VIRGIN WIFE (#921) February 1993
HAUNTED HUSBAND (#922) March 1993
LUCKY PENNY (#945) June 1993
A WEDDING FOR EMILY (#953) August 1993

Elizabeth August's SMYTHESHIRE, MASSACHUSETTS—
This sleepy little town has plenty to keep you up at night.
Only from Silhouette Romance!

THIS SIDE OF HEAVEN

The miracle of love is waiting to be discovered in Duncan, Oklahoma! Arlene James takes you there in her new trilogy, THIS SIDE OF HEAVEN.

Begin your visit to Duncan with an emotional story of love's healing strength:

The Perfect Wedding

Rod Corley was planning a wedding that he hoped would clear his family's scandalous reputation. Luckily for Layne Harrington, Rod wasn't the groom. But would Layne's love be enough to help Rod forget the past?

Available in September,
only from

Silhouette

ROMANCE™

Silhouette Books has done it again!

Opening night in October has never been as exciting! Come watch as the curtain rises and romance flourishes when the stars of tomorrow make their debuts today!

Revel in Jodi O'Donnell's STILL SWEET ON HIM—
Silhouette Romance #969
...as Callie Farrell's renovation of the family homestead leads her straight into the arms of teenage crush Drew Barnett!

Tingle with Carol Devine's BEAUTY AND THE BEASTMASTER—
Silhouette Desire #816
...as legal eagle Amanda Tarkington is carried off by wrestler Bram Masterson!

Thrill to Elyn Day's A BED OF ROSES—
Silhouette Special Edition #846
...as Dana Whitaker's body and soul are healed by sexy physical therapist Michael Gordon!

Believe when Kylie Brant's McLAIN'S LAW—
Silhouette Intimate Moments #528
...takes you into detective Connor McLain's life as he falls for psychic—and suspect—Michele Easton!

Catch the classics of tomorrow—*premiering* today—
only from ⍦ *Silhouette*

SILHOUETTE'S FATHER OF THE YEAR CONTEST
OFFICIAL RULES

Here's how to enter:

1. On one side of an 8½" × 11" piece of paper to which you have attached a photograph of your father, hand print or type your name, address, the name of your father, and in 200 words or fewer, tell us why your father is so fabulous.

2. Mail your completed entry (limit one per envelope) via first-class mail to: SILHOUETTE'S FATHER OF THE YEAR CONTEST, 3010 Walden Avenue, P.O. Box 9046, Buffalo, NY 14269-9046 if mailing from U.S., or SILHOUETTE'S FATHER OF THE YEAR CONTEST, P.O. Box 613, Fort Erie, Ontario L2A 5X3, if mailing from Canada. All entries must be received no later than 9/30/93. No responsibility is assumed for lost, late or misdirected mail.

3. Entries will be judged on the basis of sensitivity—60%—and appropriateness—40%—of the essay. All entries and photographs become the property of Harlequin Enterprises, Ltd. and may be used for advertising, merchandising or publicity purposes. No correspondence will be answered. Only one prize will be awarded. The winner will be selected no later than 10/31/93 and notified by mail. Prize consists of a Fab Dad Sweatshirt and Book Collection (value: $75 U.S.).

4. Contest open to residents of U.S. and Canada. Employees of Torstar Corporation, D.L. Blair, Inc., their affiliates, subsidiaries, advertising, printing and promotional agencies and members of their immediate families are not eligible. Tax liability on prize is the sole responsibility of winner. Contest is void wherever prohibited and is subject to all Federal, State and local laws and regulations.

5. Potential winner must execute and return an Affidavit of Eligibility and Publicity Release within 30 days of notification or an alternate winner may be selected. Entry and acceptance of prize offered constitutes permission to use winner's/father's name and/or likeness, for purposes of advertising and trade on behalf of Harlequin Enterprises, Ltd., without further compensation unless prohibited by law.

6. For the name of the winner (available after 11/30/93), send a self-addressed, stamped envelope to: Silhouette's Father of the Year Contest Winner, P.O. Box 4200, Blair, NE 68009.

SRFORUL

Now you can enter your

in Silhouette Romance's
"FATHER OF THE YEAR" contest
and win great prizes for both of you!

Simply write to Silhouette, telling us why your father is so fabulous,
and include a photo of him. Entry coupons and details can be found
inside any of the June, July or August FABULOUS FATHER titles. The
winning father will have his photo placed in the inside back cover of
the June 1994 Fabulous Father title and the winning letter will be
placed in the back pages of the same title. In addition, the FATHER
OF THE YEAR will receive a great FABULOUS FATHER sweatshirt and
the submitter will receive a complete set of 1993 FAB DAD books to
enjoy.

To enter the Silhouette Romance FATHER OF THE YEAR Contest, fill out the coupon below
with *your* name, address, and zip or postal code and enclose it with your letter and photo to:

In the U.S.	In Canada
Silhouette Romance	Silhouette Romance
FATHER OF THE YEAR Contest	FATHER OF THE YEAR Contest
3010 Walden Avenue	P.O. Box 613
P.O. Box 9046	Fort Erie, Ontario
Buffalo, NY 14269-9046	L2A 5X3

Your Name: _____
Address: _____
City: _____ State/Prov.: _____
Zip/Postal: _____
Your Father's Name: _____
Place where you purchased your Fabulous Father title: _____

KAZ

(Contest entry deadline is September 30, 1993. See previous page for
full contest details.)

SRFDPOP